# FAIRY ❖ TALES

# Fairy ❖ Tales

### Told by
## Berlie Doherty

### Illustrated by
## Jane Ray

## Walker Books
### and subsidiaries
LONDON · BOSTON · SYDNEY · AUCKLAND

*F*airy stories are enchanted dreams. We remember them as if they had been sung to us while we were under the spell of a long deep sleep, and when we hear them again we think, Ah yes! I know this from long ago. That is because they are hundreds and hundreds of years old, and have been told a million times before to children just like you.

Every time the stories are told, the tellers add a little bit of themselves – a colour here, a jewel there, a sigh or a secret laugh or a song that wasn't there before. But they must never, never change what actually happens, because the magic of fairy stories is just right. There are patterns that run through them all, because they have always been known to be the right patterns. So beauty means goodness and goodness is rewarded, and love is the highest reward. Evil is wrong and will always be punished.

These are among the loveliest stories in the world. When my editor, Wendy Boase, asked me if I would work with Jane Ray and tell the stories in my own voice, I felt she was giving me the most precious task I had ever undertaken. I wanted to tell them in a way that would always sing for her.

These enchanted dreams are for Wendy

Berlie & Jane

First published 2000 by Walker Books Ltd
87 Vauxhall Walk, London SE11 5HJ

This edition published 2018

2 4 6 8 10 9 7 5 3 1

Text © 2000 Berlie Doherty
Illustrations © 2000 Jane Ray

The right of Berlie Doherty and Jane Ray to be identified as author
and illustrator respectively of this work has been asserted by them in
accordance with the Copyright, Designs and Patents Act 1988

This book has been typeset in Palatino

Printed in China

British Library Cataloguing in Publication Data:
a catalogue record for this book is available from the British Library

ISBN 978-1-4063-7989-1

www.walker.co.uk

# THE ❖ TALES

# CINDERELLA

There was once a girl who lived with her father and his new wife and her two daughters. Her mother had died, and the new wife was jealous because the girl missed her mother so much, and because she was prettier than her own daughters. She tried to hide her away at the bottom of the house. And the sisters had such ugly hearts that they treated the girl as if she was their servant. They came to be known as the ugly sisters.

The girl had to do everything for them, and never got any thanks for it. All she had to wear was a ragged grey dress, and at night when her work was done, she had to sleep on the hearth among the ashes and the cinders. And so she became known as Cinderella.

One day Cinderella's father was going on a journey, and he asked his three daughters what they would like him to bring back for them.

"Oh, some glittery gold to wear round my neck!" said the oldest.

"Oh, some sparkly jewels to match my eyes!" said the second.

The father smiled fondly and said to Cinderella, "And what about you?"

"I would like the first twig that brushes against your hat as you ride," said Cinderella.

Her sisters laughed in scorn.

"The girl's an idiot!" the stepmother said.

"She doesn't even deserve a present!"

So when the father came home again he had gold and jewels and a twig from a hazel tree in his bag, and straight away Cinderella ran outside with her twig and stuck it in the earth on her mother's grave, and wept over it.

Every day, if Cinderella had a little time for herself in between all her chores, she would steal out to the twig and nourish it with her tears, and it wasn't long before something wonderful happened. The hazel twig started to grow. It began to put out spindly little branches, and buds sprouted on the branches, and green leaves unfurled from the buds. It became a tree. Its leaves danced and fluttered in the wind, and wrens and blackbirds and thrushes and turtle-doves all settled in its branches and sang to her.

Soon after this had happened there came an announcement that the Prince of the Realm was to hold a three-day feast, with a magnificent ball on each of the three nights, and that at the end of the three days he was going to choose his bride. Imagine the excitement at Cinderella's house when the invitations arrived!

"At last, at last!" the stepmother said to her husband. "He's bound to choose one of our daughters!"

The two ugly sisters were full of it. It was all they could talk about, and they squabbled all the time over which of them was most likely to be chosen by the prince. They ordered Cinderella to make ball-gowns for them, and they paraded in front of the looking-glass, scowling at what they saw and blaming Cinderella for everything.

"Too long!"

"Too short!"

"Too tight!"

"Too loose!"

"Too plain!"

"Too flouncy!"

"Can't you do anything right!" her stepmother shouted.

When there was no more material to be used up and the night of the first ball was upon them, they told Cinderella that her efforts would have to do. Not a word of thanks, of course.

"Now you can do our hair," they said. "Make us look beautiful, and be quick about it!"

They were asking the impossible, of course, but Cinderella did her best, and when all this was done, she said to her stepmother, "What can I wear to the ball?"

Her stepmother was so astonished that she nearly forgot how to speak. "You!" she said. "Who said anything about you going to the ball?"

"But the invitation was for all of us. Please let me go!" Cinderella turned to her father. "Please let me!"

And this is what the stepmother did, to keep her quiet. She picked up a bowl of rice and flung it into the ashes of the fire. "Pick out all those grains of rice," she told her, "and then you may go to the ball." She went upstairs with her two daughters, and they put on their ball-gowns.

Cinderella ran out of the kitchen to her hazel tree and called up to it,

*"Hazel tree, hazel tree,*
*Will you help me?"*

Instantly there was a chirruping and cooing and a fluttering of wings, and her wrens and her thrushes and blackbirds and her turtle-doves all flew down to her. They picked and pecked through the ashes and in no time at all there was a bowl of clean rice grains with all the ashes shaken off.

Singing with excitement, Cinderella ran to show her stepmother. "Now I can go to the ball!" she said.

Her stepmother didn't even look at the bowl of rice in Cinderella's hands. "Don't be ridiculous! In that tatty dress! You can't even dance! It's out of the question."

Cinderella begged and pleaded so much that this is what the stepmother did. She took *two* bowls of lentils and threw them into the ashes. "Pick those out, clean enough to eat, and you can go to the ball," she said, and she and her daughters started putting on their gloves and their dancing slippers.

So once more Cinderella ran out of the kitchen to her hazel tree and called up to its branches,

> *"Hazel tree, hazel tree,*
> *Will you help me?"*

Instantly there was a chirruping and a fluttering of wings and her wrens and her thrushes and blackbirds and her turtle-doves picked and pecked through the ashes to find all the lentils, and shook them till they were clean enough to eat.

Full of joy, Cinderella ran out of the kitchen with the bowls. Her stepmother and sisters were just about to step into the carriage. The horse was stamping his hooves, ready to be off. "Wait!" Cinderella called. "I've done it! I can go now!"

But her mother and her sisters laughed, and didn't even look at the bowls of lentils. "Look at you! You're a bundle of rags! How can you possibly go to the ball?"

Cinderella clung on to her father's hand. "Please let me go!" But her stepmother took up the reins and the carriage swept away.

Cinderella was left alone in the house. Sad and sighing, she went out to her hazel tree and sat underneath it.

*"Hazel tree, hazel tree,*
*If only you could help me."*

She heard a fluttering as if all the leaves were unfurling at once, and the birds of the tree flew down carrying a silver dress and slippers that glittered like stars. Cinderella put them on, and ran to the ball.

The palace was glowing with coloured streamers and candlelight. Beautiful ladies swayed and danced in their gorgeous butterfly gowns. Nobody recognized Cinderella when she came in, but everybody gazed at her because she was the most beautiful person there. The prince came to

her straight away and asked her to dance with him, and never left her side all evening.

When she saw her father leave she said she must go.

"Let me take you home then," the prince begged her, but she slipped away from him, not wanting him to know who she was. He followed after her, anxious not to lose sight of her, and she ran into the house where her father kept his doves and closed the door behind her. Then she ran through another door and out to her tree, and put her silver dress and slippers there for the birds to hide. The prince called her father out and begged him to open up the dove-house for him, but by this time Cinderella was lying in the hearth in her dirty grey dress, and nobody knew what had happened.

There was another ball the next night, but this time Cinderella said nothing to her stepmother. She helped her sisters to get dressed and then, when they had all gone to the ball, she went out to her hazel tree.

> *"Hazel tree, hazel tree,*
> *Will you help me?"*

There was a rustling of leaves and the birds of the tree flew down to her, and this time her dress and her slippers shimmered like the moon. Cinderella put them on and ran to the ball, and again no one recognized her for who she was, and again the prince danced with her all night. When she left to go home she knew that he was following her, and when she was near her father's house she ran into the garden and hid in a pear tree.

"Come down!" the prince called to her in despair. He went to her father and told him that the beautiful princess who was at the ball had hidden in the tree. The father was puzzled to think that twice the princess should hide in the grounds of his own house. He chopped down the tree, but there was nobody there, because Cinderella had taken her shimmering dress and slippers back to the hazel tree, and was lying among the ashes of the hearth in her old grey rags.

On the night of the third ball she went out again to the hazel tree.

> *"Hazel tree, hazel tree,*
> *Will you help me?"*

And the birds fluttered down to her with a dress and slippers that were as golden as the sun itself,

and Cinderella had never looked more beautiful. The prince danced with her all night, and this time, he told himself, he would not lose her. When midnight struck and she saw that her father had left she tried to slip away. The prince ran after her instantly, calling to her to wait for him, and in her great haste she dropped one of her golden slippers. He picked it up and held it next to his heart.

"Whoever this fits, I shall marry," he said.

Next day he visited all the daughters of all the houses to have them try on the golden slipper, but it was so small and delicate that it fitted nobody. When he arrived at Cinderella's house the two ugly sisters were rubbing perfumed oils between their toes to make them smell nice.

"You have such lovely feet," their mother told them. "He's bound to marry one of you."

CINDERELLA

They scowled at each other, but when the prince came in they were full of smiles and dimples.

The oldest one tried the slipper first, but tug and push as she might she just couldn't get her foot into it. "It's my big toe!" she moaned to her mother. "It won't go in."

"Chop it off then!" her mother hissed, and handed her a knife. "You won't need it when you're married to the prince." So she did, and the slipper fitted. But as she was riding back to the palace with the prince they passed Cinderella's hazel tree, and all the birds set up a frenzied chanting to the prince to look at her slipper.

The prince stopped the carriage and looked, and sure enough, the slipper was full of blood. He took the girl back to her mother and asked to see her sister. She did her very best to get the slipper to fit, but there didn't seem to be any chance of that.

"It's nearly there," she whispered to her mother, gasping and red-faced with the effort, "but I can't get my heel in."

"Push, you fool," her mother said, and rammed the shoe on so hard that her daughter's foot started to bleed. Still, the shoe was on, and the prince took her for his bride.

But as they were driving to the palace past the hazel tree the birds set up such a riot of chanting that the prince stopped the carriage again and saw the blood staining the heel of the sister's white stocking, so he turned the carriage round and took her back home.

"You haven't got another daughter, have you?" he said to the father.

"No," said the father, and Cinderella stood up

from the ashes. "Well, only Cinderella."

"But look at the state of her," the stepmother said. "She'd never make a bride for you."

But Cinderella stepped forward and curtsied to the prince and took the slipper from his hand, and it slid on to her foot so easily that he knew it was hers. Then he looked at her face and knew that she was the girl who had danced with him for three whole nights; even though her hair was matted with ash and her clothes were stained and torn, he knew her.

The stepmother and the ugly sisters set up a great howl of rage and all the birds of the hazel tree flew down and pecked and picked at them until they sobbed for mercy and forgiveness.

But Cinderella and the prince saw nothing of this. He went down on one knee and asked her if she would marry him; and Cinderella said *yes*.

# THE SLEEPING BEAUTY IN THE FOREST

One day a queen was walking alone in her beautiful rose garden. She had everything she could wish for except the thing she wanted most. As she passed a briar rose bush she heard a pitiful fluttering and saw a golden bird trapped in its branches. "Oh, poor thing," she said. She hurried to free it, and as soon as she parted the branches the bird lifted its gleaming golden wings and flew out of the bush.

"You will have what you wish for," it sang to her, and the queen hurried back to the castle, full of joy.

And it was true. Before the year was over she had given birth to a baby daughter.

"I'd like to call her Briar Rose, after the bush in the garden," she said.

Well, the king thought it was a strange name to call a child, but he was so happy that he agreed. "We must have a great christening feast for her."

And the queen said, "She's a magic child, remember. I think we should invite the fairies."

So the invitations were sent out to all the fairies in the kingdom, but by mistake one of them was left out. It was a terrible mistake. Of all the fairies she was the most powerful. She was known as the Fairy of Shadows. She was a weaver of wicked spells.

On the day of the christening the air in the castle shimmered as if it was lit by stars, and a strange and wonderful humming came from nowhere, and then all of a sudden the hall was full of fairies, all bringing gifts for the baby Princess Briar Rose: bells for her music, flowers for her beauty, crystal water for her dancing – those sort of presents, fairy presents. The last fairy of all was just about to lay her gift in the cradle when there came a rushing of icy wind. All the candles flickered and the curtains floated like the waves of the sea. The air went cold and still. And there was the Fairy of Shadows, her eyes glowing like rubies in her white face. She stared at every one of them in turn, and nobody moved.

"Why was I not invited to the christening?" she demanded.

The king and queen rushed forward, begging forgiveness, but she swept past them as if they were invisible. She walked straight to the cradle where the baby Briar Rose lay fast asleep.

"I was not invited," said the Fairy of Shadows, "but all the same I have brought a gift."

From inside her cloak she drew a wreath of black flowers and tossed it on to the cradle. "This is my gift," she hissed. "On your fifteenth birthday you will prick your finger on the spindle of a spinning wheel. And you will die." And with that, the wicked fairy swirled her black cloaks around herself in a cloud of rippling thunder, and she disappeared.

The king and queen wrung their hands in despair. "Can't you do something?" they begged.

But the fairies shook their heads and looked away. "She is the most powerful fairy of all. Nothing can undo her magic," they said.

And then the youngest fairy stepped forward.

"Wait," she said. "I haven't given my gift to the princess yet. It's true, I can't undo the magic of the Fairy of Shadows. But I can weaken it. Princess Briar Rose will prick her finger on her fifteenth birthday. But she won't die. Instead she will sleep for a hundred years. You will all sleep with her, every creature in this castle. She can only be wakened with a kiss. That is all I can do."

And the fairies turned into specks of golden pollen and blew away.

The queen lifted her baby out of the cradle and hugged her close. "What kind of a future is that?" she wept. "To sleep for a hundred years!"

The king put his arms round his wife and begged her to stop crying and to listen to him. "It would be a terrible thing, but it won't happen," he promised her. "I will order every spinning wheel in the country to be brought to the castle and burnt. It's so simple."

And that was exactly what he did. A huge bonfire was lit outside the castle and all the spinning wheels in the country were brought out and flung into it. Everybody was eager to help.

> *"Save the princess!"* they sang.
> *"Let the wicked fairy do her worst;*
> *We'll burn away her evil curse!"*

But the wicked fairy watched from the shadows and laughed to herself.

❖ ❖ ❖

Briar Rose had everything that the fairies wished for her; she was beautiful and clever, strong and healthy, wise and good. She could dance like a dragonfly and sing like a skylark, and what was more, everybody loved her. Her fifteenth birthday came, and her parents decided to hold a big party to celebrate it.

"And we've invited all the young princes," they told her. "They all want to meet you, Briar Rose."

"What for?"

"Why, to marry you, of course. One of those handsome princes may choose you to be his bride."

"Marry me! I don't want to get married! I don't want to meet any horrible handsome princes," Briar Rose said. "I just want to play with my friends in the castle."

But it was too late. They could hear the jingling of the approaching carriages, and the fanfare of trumpets announcing the arrival of the young princes. The king and queen hurried to the great

hall to get ready to welcome them, and Briar Rose decided that there was only one thing she could do to avoid the horrible handsome princes. She would have to hide. She ran out of the castle and into the gardens, and there she found a tower that she had never noticed before. She pushed open the door and stepped inside. She could hear the sound of something going *creak! creak! creak!* She climbed the shallow stairs to find out what was making the sound. There in the cobwebby attic she saw something she had never seen in her life before. It was a spinning wheel.

An old lady was spinning black strands of wool like the legs of giant spiders, and when she saw Briar Rose watching she didn't stop for a moment. She raised her hand in its black fingerless mitten and she said, "Would you like to try? Come here,

my dear. Sit down beside me and I'll show you what to do."

Slowly, slowly, because she was a little bit afraid, Briar Rose approached the old woman and sat down beside her. The old woman smiled, and guided her hand, and as soon as Briar Rose touched the spindle she gave a gasp of pain, because it was as if the point had pierced her heart. Three drops of blood glistened on her finger. Instantly she fell asleep. The old woman swirled her black cloaks around her and disappeared.

The clock in the great hall of the castle stopped ticking. And the king and queen fell asleep; the serving-maid in the kitchen, the stable-lad and his horses, the butler and the parlour-maid, all yawned and slept. The chamber-maid fell into the bed she was making, the cook nodded into his cake bowl,

the dogs curled up on the stairs, the cats and the mice lay down side by side, the candle flames fluttered and went out. The castle, and all its people, fell into a deep, deep sleep.

Around the castle there grew a forest that was so high and so deep that no light penetrated through. No birds flew there, no animals moved. Twined around every branch of every tree were briars, with thorns as sharp as needles. And so it remained for a hundred years.

News spread of the enchanted castle and the beautiful princess who slept inside it. Knights and princes came from all round the world and tried to fight their way through the trees to rescue her, but the forest was too thick and the thorns too sharp. They all died, every one, ripped to shreds. One day a young prince was walking near the forest and a golden bird flew over his head and dropped a feather. The prince bent to pick it up, and the feather turned into a key in his hand. "What can it be?" he asked. An old man was passing by, and he looked at the key and told the prince a story that his grandfather had told him, many years before. "Deep in that forest there's a castle, and by the castle is a tower. In the tower is a room, and in that room is a bed. And on that bed a princess lies. She's been there for a hundred years. Not dead, young sir. Sleeping. That's the story I've heard. Go, sir, rescue her."

The old man went on his way, and the prince stood with the key in his hand not knowing what to do. Tattered rags fluttered from the branches of the forest trees, all that was left of the brave princes who had tried before him.

"I daren't go in there!" he said. "It's so dark and deep." Yet he thought of the princess who had lain under a spell for a hundred years, and who would never wake up unless she was rescued.

"I'll do it!" he said. "I'll try." He lifted up his sword to hack his way through, and instantly the golden bird flew down as if to show him the way. Roses grew on the briars, and the branches parted to let the sunlight through. The great trees swayed to let him pass, and there in the distance he could see the great castle with a tower standing near by. He went to the tower and climbed the stairs. He opened the door with his golden key, and there was the room, and there was the bed, and there was the princess lying on it, as fresh as if she had just fallen asleep that very minute.

"How beautiful she is!" the prince said, and

without thinking he bent down and kissed her. And Princess Briar Rose opened her eyes.

The great clock in the castle started to tick. The king and queen yawned and stretched. The serving-maid in the kitchen, the stable-lad tending the horses, the butler, the parlour-maid, all rubbed their eyes. The chamber-maid jumped out of the bed and carried on making it, the cook jerked his head out of the cake bowl and licked his lips,

the dogs strolled down the stairs, the cats chased the mice, and the candle flames flickered back to life.

"You don't look as if you're over a hundred," the young prince said.

"A hundred!" Briar Rose laughed. "It's my fifteenth birthday!"

She stood up, and was so beautiful that the young prince fell on to his knees.

"Will you marry me?" he asked.

And Princess Briar Rose smiled at him and said *yes*.

# Beauty and the Beast

There was a merchant who had three daughters and three sons. The youngest of them all was known as Beauty, and her sisters were jealous of her and treated her just as if she was their servant. They made her wash and cook while they went off to parties. But Beauty didn't mind. She was her father's favourite child; she loved him and he loved her, and that made up for everything. Many a young man came asking her to marry him, but she always said no. She loved her father too much to leave him.

One winter the merchant fell on hard times. One by one his ships were lost at sea in terrible storms, and all his wealth went with them. He had to sell their beautiful house and move into a much smaller one. The sons had to work in the fields, and the daughters to take in washing. The older girls hated this so much that they lazed in bed till ten o'clock every morning, knowing that Beauty would have got up at four to make sure the work was done. She did it willingly. It hurt her to see how distressed their father was, and she would do anything to make him happy again.

Then, one day, he received news that made him prance round the garden with joy, as if he was a young man again.

"My last ship has come home!" he sang, waving a letter at them. "We're rich again!"

He saddled his horse at once and set off to the port to sort out his business affairs. His daughters ran alongside him as far as the village well.

"Bring me lots of silk gowns!" the oldest one said.

"Bring me a little monkey!" said the middle one.

"What about you, Beauty?" The merchant laughed, full of high spirits.

"Oh," she said. "Bring me a rose, Father."

The sisters laughed at her and the merchant went on his way, singing because the morning was bright and full of promise. But by the end of the day all his happiness had vanished away. The news he had been sent was false. Far from having a ship full of merchandise, he had nothing at all. His last ship had sunk. He was completely penniless. He turned his horse for home, sad and weary though he was. It could be that he fell asleep at the reins, who knows? Anyway, he lost his way. There was a terrific snow-storm, hail came lashing down and thunder roared about him. He saw a mansion lit up in a flash of lightning and rode up towards the huge wrought-iron gates.

"Perhaps I could shelter here," he said aloud, and instantly the great gates swung open. He rode in, and the gates swung shut behind him. It was the same when he reached the mansion house. The door of the stable swung open, and he dismounted and let his horse trot in for shelter and food. He climbed the steps of the mansion and was just about to pull the bell when the great studded door swung back. He stepped inside, and it was closed behind him. There was no one to be seen, yet he had the sensation of eyes peering at him. A bright fire sprang up in the grate; unseen hands lifted his soaked overcoat from his shoulders and his hat from his head and his gloves from his hands. He looked about him, and there was no one there.

A comfortable chair was pulled up to the fire, and he felt himself being guided towards it, and he sank down and fell asleep.

When he woke up a table had been placed at his side with tasty-smelling food steaming in a silver bowl and red wine glowing in a crystal goblet. There was still no sign of his host, but the merchant ate and drank thankfully. It was a long time since he had eaten so well. When he had finished, the table was lifted away out of sight. The great clock chimed twelve, and one by one the candles were blown out, yet one remained, as if to light his way upstairs. The merchant stood up, yawning, and climbed the stairs. A door opened, and there was a bed freshly made, the covers turned back neatly. He knew it was meant for him, and within seconds of climbing into it he was asleep.

Next morning it was as if the storm had never been. The sun streamed through the windows. The merchant found that fine new clothes had been put out for him, and that his breakfast had been set out. He called for his host, but no one came. Yet still he had the sensation of being watched from some hidden place. He went outside to fetch his horse from the stable, and saw a garden full of sweet-smelling roses, even though it was still winter and snow laced the trees. He thought at once about Beauty, and decided to pick a rose for her before he left. He put out his hand and plucked one.

At once he heard the roar of a wild animal and dropped the rose in his terror. The bushes were clawed aside and there in front of him a hideous creature reared up on his hind legs, lashing out as if he was going to rip the merchant up into tiny shreds.

"How dare you pick my roses!" he snarled. "I have given you food and shelter willingly. How dare you steal my roses!"

The merchant flung himself on to his knees, weak with fear. "Forgive me. Please forgive me, my lord," he begged.

"I am not 'my lord'. I am the Beast. You will die for this." The Beast dropped down on to all fours and prowled round the merchant, baring his teeth and growling.

"I beg you to let me go. I only picked the rose for my daughter. All my sons and daughters will be watching out for me. At least let me say good-bye to them."

"Go back to your sons and daughters," the Beast roared. "But within one month you must return. Either you or one of your daughters must die.

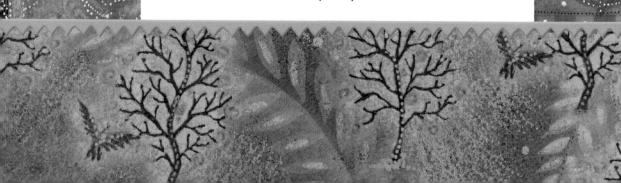

That is my bargain."

"I promise I'll come back," the merchant said, heavy with dread. Then he scrambled on to his horse and galloped home as if the wind was carrying him.

"I'm only with you for a short while," he told his sons and daughters. "I have come to say good-bye." And he told them the strange story of the mansion and the unseen servants, and the beautiful garden full of sweet roses in the snow. He gave Beauty her rose, and last of all he told them about the Beast, and of the promise he had made.

"I must go back to him," he said. "And you will never see me again, children."

"Let me go instead," Beauty said at once.

"Yes, let her go," the sisters said. "It was all her fault for asking for a rose."

At the end of the month Beauty and her father both went to the Beast's mansion. The huge gates swung open for them, and they went in slowly and full of fear. Again there was no one to be seen, and yet they both had the feeling that unseen eyes were watching them.

"Leave me now," Beauty said.

"How can I leave you here?" her father asked.

"You must," said Beauty, and sadly her father said goodbye to her and went back home.

Beauty found that wonderful things had been prepared for her: beautiful food, fine clothes, gorgeous jewels, yet she had no heart for any of them. She ate alone on her first evening, served by invisible hands. She felt eyes watching her, and knew that the Beast was with her. She could smell the stink of blood on him, and the foul reek of his breath; she could hear the scratch of his claws on the tiles, and when she turned to look at him she nearly fainted with fear.

"Do you have everything you need, Beauty?" he asked her.

"Yes, thank you," she said, wishing with all her heart that he would go away. She couldn't bring herself to look at him again.

"I won't trouble you," he said. "But I should like to see you every day. May I come when you are dining, just to watch you eat?"

"You are the master," said Beauty. "I must do as you wish."

"No. I must do as *you* wish," said the Beast. "Will you please permit me, Beauty?"

So she said yes, and the next night when she was dining she shuddered to hear the scrape of

his claws on the ground, and the rasp of his breathing behind her ear. At the end of her meal he put his paw over her trembling hand. "Beauty, will you marry me?" he asked.

"No!" she screamed. She pushed him away and ran to her room, where she flung herself on her bed and sobbed for home. She was trapped with the Beast. It was quite clear that he had no intention of killing her, but she might as well be dead, she thought. Every night he came to her at nine, and every night he asked her to marry him, and always her answer was the same. But whenever he spoke there was such a deep sorrowing in his voice that she began to pity him.

"I am the Beast, and you are afraid of me," he said. "Forgive me."

"I'm not afraid of you now," Beauty said. "But

I can't marry you."

"No," he said sadly.

"But I can be your friend," she told him. It was true. She began to look forward to his coming every evening. She was bored and lonely when he wasn't there. In a strange way that she couldn't understand, Beauty grew to like the Beast. But he was a beast. He killed the wild creatures in the woods around his mansion, and would sometimes have their blood on his paws and around his mouth when he came to see her. "Forgive me," he would say to her. "This is how I am."

One day the Beast gave her a mirror as a present, but when she looked into it she did not see her own reflection. She saw her father lying in bed in a poor room, and he looked old and sad and ill. Beauty ran to the Beast and begged him to let her go home.

"You want to leave me, Beauty?" he said, and his voice was so full of sadness that she felt tears rising in her.

"No, I don't want to leave you. Not for ever," she said. "But I want to be with my father too."

"Go to him," said the Beast. "But come back to me in a week. I can't live without you, Beauty."

So Beauty looked into the mirror again, and said "Father," and in that very instant she was back in the old house and standing at her father's bedside.

"Beauty!" he gasped. "Is it really you? I thought you were dead."

He sat up and laughed with joy. He had been wasting away with sadness, but the sight of his favourite daughter was all he needed to make him well and happy again. "Help me out of this

bed," he told her. "I don't need it now."

His daughters and sons were working in the garden when they saw their father walking towards them on the arm of a beautiful stranger.

"Who's that fine lady?" the brothers marvelled.

"That's no fine lady. It's Beauty!" the oldest sister snapped.

"Just look at her, done up like a queen!" the middle sister said. "Who does she think she is!"

But Beauty was glad to give them her jewels and her silk gown. "I don't need them," she told them. "All I need is to see my father well and happy."

"Promise me you won't ever go away again," he asked her.

"I can't promise that, Father. The Beast wants me to go back in a week."

"But you don't have to!" her oldest brother said.

"We'll kill him for you."

When he said that, Beauty went pale and her eyes brimmed with tears. They all looked at her strangely.

"Why," said her father, "what's this, Beauty? I do believe you have grown fond of the Beast!"

But she turned away and couldn't speak for the odd sadness that filled her heart.

All the same, they begged her to stay with them. Her father was well and strong, but he said he would take to his bed immediately if she were to leave him again. Beauty had taken up her tasks around the house and in the fields so willingly that her sisters were determined to make her stay so they wouldn't have to work any more. On the day she was due to leave they squeezed onion juice into their eyes to make themselves cry. "Don't go! Please don't go, Beauty!" they begged her, and

Beauty was moved by their tears. She felt as if her heart was being torn in two.

So she stayed, but every night she dreamed of the Beast. Nearly a week later she picked up her mirror, and instead of her reflection she saw him. His eyes were closed, and he was slumped on the ground, too weak to move. She gave a cry of horror. "Beast!" she sobbed. "Don't die! Oh please don't die!" And instantly she was running through the great wrought-iron gates of the mansion, running through the gardens, running through the sweet-smelling rose bower and into the wild part where the Beast liked to hunt.

"Beast!" she called. "Where are you? Oh, where are you, Beast?"

At last she saw him stretched out in the long grass. His eyes were closed, and he was as still

as death. She ran to him and cradled his head in her arms. "Don't die. Please don't die!" she sobbed. "I love you, Beast."

And when she said that, the Beast opened his eyes. His rough coat fell away from him and he stood up, young and strong; a man.

"Beauty, I was under a spell," he said. "And you have broken it with your love. Will you marry me?"

And Beauty said *yes*.

They had a magnificent wedding, and the merchant and his sons were given homes in the grounds of the mansion. The sisters were turned into statues and placed in the rose garden, and there they stayed until they were truly sorry, and that was a long, long time.

But Beauty and her prince lived happily until the end of their days.

# RUMPELSTILTSKIN

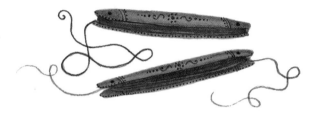

Once upon a time there was a poor weaver who had a beautiful daughter. When she worked beside him spinning her thread, her hair shone like strands of gold, and her father would look at her and sigh.

"Daughter, you're much too beautiful to marry a poor man. You deserve to be married to the King of the Realm and to live in great happiness."

His daughter looked at him and smiled and carried on with her spinning. "I'm happy with you, Father. And no one has asked me to marry him yet. And anyway, I'm never likely even to meet the King of the Realm!"

Now, one day the weaver and his daughter were sitting outside in the sunshine at work, because their cottage was cold and damp and gloomy inside, with walls that were five feet thick and a low thatched roof that sank over the tops of the tiny windows. They were enjoying the birdsong when they heard the clattering of hooves and some men on horseback drew up. They were dressed very grand indeed in silks and fine cloth, which the weaver admired. And it was obvious that the grandest of them all was admiring the weaver's daughter, and the way the sunlight gleamed in her long golden hair.

"You think she is beautiful?" the weaver asked,

thinking to himself how wonderful it would be if this man wanted to marry his daughter.

"I do," said the fine young man. "I think she's more beautiful than any girl I have ever seen."

"More than that," the cunning weaver said. "She is the cleverest. She can spin straw into gold."

"Well," laughed the young man, "I would like to believe that. Perhaps your daughter would come with me and show me. If what you say is true, old man, I will ask your daughter to be my wife. May I take her to my castle?"

It was only then that the weaver realized that he was talking to the king himself. He fluttered round his daughter. "Go on," he whispered, tripping over bales of cloth in his excitement. "Go with His Majesty before he changes his mind."

"But Father," she whispered back, "how can I? You know I can't spin straw into gold!"

"Ssh!" her father whispered back. "Never mind. He's half in love with you already. Off you go!"

And because she loved her father, she went. He stood at his cottage door and waved goodbye to her, and tears of hope streamed down into his beard. "My daughter will marry the king," he said.

And maybe his words were heard by the creatures of the wood, and maybe they weren't.

As soon as they arrived at the castle the young king put the girl into a room, and all that was in it was a spinning wheel and a mound of straw.

"Let's see what you can do, because I would like to marry you," the king said. "But how can I marry a poor weaver's daughter?" And he closed the door on her.

The girl stared gloomily at the straw. "His Majesty will be putting me on a horse and sending me home again tomorrow," she said. And a bit later she was still staring at the straw. "He won't be sending me home on a horse. He will be making me walk barefoot and ashamed." And a bit later she was still staring at the straw, and she said, "He won't be sending me home at all. He will be putting me in the dungeon for lying to him, and I'll never see my father again. Oh, my poor father!"

"Now stop that crying!" She heard a strange, croaky voice, and looked around to see a little hump-backed man with skin that was crumpled like an old dry apple. "What will you give me if I spin this straw into gold for you?"

"Can you really do that?"

"I said I could," the little man snapped, holding out his hand.

The girl took off her necklace and gave it to him, and he told her to close her eyes, and she fell asleep to the sound of the hum of the spinning wheel. And when she woke up, the little man had gone and in the corner of the room where the straw had been there was now a heap of gold.

"This is wonderful," the king said when he saw it. "But can you do it again?"

He ordered more straw and left her in her room, and the girl was more downhearted than ever. She thought of her father in his lonely cottage waiting for news of her.

"How can I possibly spin this straw into gold?" she said. "Oh, my poor father. Will I ever see him again?"

"Stop that!" she heard the little man say, and there he was, standing next to her and holding out his hand. "We did it once, we'll do it twice."

So the girl pulled off her ring and gave it to him, and closed her eyes, and fell asleep to the sound of the spinning wheel humming. And when she woke up, the little man had gone and so had the pile of straw. And in its place there was a heap of gold.

When he saw it the king was even more delighted with her. "Your father was right," he said. "You are as clever as you are beautiful. But before I ask you to marry me, I must be sure that you can do it a third time." He ordered more straw to be brought to her room, and he closed the door and left it there.

And this time the girl was in deep despair. Night came down, and no sign of the little man.

The moon came up, no sign of the little man. Dawn began to creep across the sky, no sign of the little man. "Oh, my poor father," she sobbed.

"Stop that!" There was the little man, standing by her side and holding out his hand. "We did it once, we did it twice, we'll do it thrice."

"But I haven't anything else to give you," the girl said. "You've had my necklace, you've had my ring, and I haven't anything else."

"I'll spin your straw into gold," the little man said. "And you will marry the king. And when your first child is born, you will give him to me. That is my bargain. Do you agree?"

Outside the cockerel crowed. Day was coming. "Yes, yes," said the girl, and she closed her eyes.

And it was just as the little man with the crumpled apple skin had said. The king was so pleased to see that the straw had been turned into gold that he asked the girl to marry him, and she said *yes*.

There was a wonderful wedding, and the weaver came to live in the castle grounds and to make fine cloths for his son-in-law the king, and a year later the girl gave birth to a baby boy. On the night of his christening the girl sat in her room singing her baby to sleep.

"Stop that!" said a voice, and there at her side was the little man, holding out his hands. "I've come for my child," he said.

"Please, please don't take him away from me," she begged.

"You will have three chances," he said. "If you haven't guessed my name by the end of the third day, then the baby will be mine." And the next moment, he was gone.

The girl thought all night and all next day; she asked everyone she met what their names were, she sent out the king's servants to collect names, and nothing seemed right. That night, the little man appeared just as he said he would.

"Know my name?" he croaked.

She thought she might as well try the most obvious ones first.

"Humpty-back?" she suggested.

"No!" he snapped.

"Shrivel-skin?"

"No, no!" He stamped his foot on the ground.

"Stampy-foot?"

"No, no, no!" And he stamped and hopped round the room. And next thing, he had gone.

The girl sent the servants even further, and they all came back with names that didn't seem right.

And at midnight, the little man came again.

"Know my name?"

This time she thought she would try the least likely names. She began with, "Harry Handsome?"

"No!" He smiled.

"Gilbert Golden-heart!"

"No, no!" he chuckled.

"Michael the Mighty?"

"No, no, no!" And he laughed and danced round the room. "One last chance!" he croaked, and the next moment, he was gone.

Again, the girl sent out all the servants, and again they came back with names that just didn't seem right. Night came, and the last servant came home to the castle. He was the groom's lad, and he ran up the stairs to her room three at a time and pounded on her door.

"I've got a story to tell you!" he panted.

"This is no time for stories!" said the girl. "Look at the time! It's nearly midnight."

"But listen!" the lad said. "I rode over the mountain and through the wood and across the river, and I came to a place I'd never seen before. I stopped to rest my horse, and there where the fox has his lair and the old owl roosts I found a little hut, and inside it I heard a croaky voice singing. I peeped through the door and there was a strange little man leaping round his fire and singing."

"And he'll be here any minute," the girl said. "Go away and let me think! The clock is beginning to strike!"

"No," said the lad. "Listen! This is the song the little man sang:

*'Oh, I can dance and Oh, I can sing!*
*Tonight I'll have the son of the king!*
*Servants look high, servants look low,*
*They won't have my secret, wherever they go;*
*Servants go back the way they came,*
*Rumpelstiltskin is my name.'"*

The clock finished striking and the lad ran back to the stable. The girl picked up her baby,

and there was the little man, standing next to her and holding out his hands.

"Know my name?" he asked.

"Could it be Lee, or Tom, or Liam?" the girl said.

"Oh no," said the little man. "Nothing like."

"Could it be Francis? Matthew? Or Geoffrey?"

"Oh no. No good. You give up, don't you? The baby's mine!"

But instead of giving him the baby, the girl began to sing:

> *"Oh, I can dance and Oh, I can sing!*
> *You'll never have the son of the king!*
> *Servants looked high, servants looked low,*
> *They found out your secret, I'll have you know;*
> *Servants came back home again,*
> *RUMPELSTILTSKIN is your name!"*

And she laughed with delight and hugged her baby boy to her.

The little man stamped so hard that his foot went right through the floor, and he went with it, and was never seen again. And the stable-lad was given a horse that was the colour of gold, and everybody lived happily to the end of their days.

# RAPUNZEL

Long, long ago a man and wife lived in a cottage that overlooked a garden belonging to a witch. They would sit at their open window at the end of the day and breathe in all the perfumes of the flowers, and gaze at the misty colours, and say how lucky they were to live there.

"If only we had a child," they said, "there would be nothing left in the world to wish for."

Now, one summer day the wife saw something in the witch's garden that took her breath away.

It was a drift of blue rapunzel flowers. "I must have some," she said to her husband. "Please, please, I must have some rapunzel to eat. Fetch me some, fetch me some or I might die. Please, please, husband, fetch me some rapunzel."

The husband was puzzled. "Are you mad?" he said. "I'd have to climb into the witch's garden to get it!"

But it seemed that his wife *was* mad with longing for the rapunzel flower. "Please, please," she begged him, "get me that rapunzel or I'll die." And at last he gave in to her. When night came he scaled the wall like a cat, plucked a handful of rapunzel and was back over the wall in less time than it takes an owl to blink. His wife made a salad of it and ate it at once.

"Was that good?" Her husband smiled.

"Yes," she said. "More please. I'd like some more. I must have some more. Please, please!" And she begged and pleaded for three whole days till he knew they would both go mad unless he fetched her some.

So when night came he scaled the wall again, quick as a mouse, and was just stooping down with his hands around a bright bunch of the plant when a shadow fell across him.

"What are you doing in my garden?"

The man froze as if he had been turned to stone. There was the witch watching him, and her eyes were as green and deep as bog-ponds.

"I was taking some rapunzel for my sick wife," he said. He was afraid for his life, yet there was no point in pretending anything else; he still had the flowers clutched in his fist. And besides, the witch could read his secret thoughts.

"Your wife is not sick." The witch smiled. "She longs for rapunzel because of the child she is bearing."

"What?" said the man, and his heart soared with joy.

"Of course you must take her some. Take as much as you want."

"Thank you, thank you." The man fell on his knees in gratitude.

But the witch's smile had turned to frost. "And when your daughter is born, give her to me. I will be her mother."

The man could hear his wife's voice, begging him to bring her the flowers at once. Frightened out of his wits, bewildered and excited all at once, he promised to do as the witch said. Then he gathered up as much rapunzel as he could and climbed the wall to his own small yard.

And, just as the witch had told him, a daughter was born to the man and his wife on the first day of spring. They could think of only one name for her, and that was Rapunzel. She hardly had time to open her eyes and gaze round at the world before the witch was at their door.

"What do you want?" said the man and his wife, with fear in their hearts.

"My child," said the witch. "I told you. I'm her mother now."

They never saw Rapunzel again. The witch loved her so much that she kept her all to herself. She wouldn't even let her play in the garden in case the man and woman watched her from their window and tried to take her back.

By the time Rapunzel was twelve years old she was so beautiful that the witch could hardly take her eyes off her. "Look at your hair!" she marvelled. "It's like a river of gold, the way it tumbles down your back. I've never seen anything like it." She fingered her own crackly hair and sighed, and then brushed Rapunzel's until it shone like the sun.

But the witch was worried in case anybody saw Rapunzel and wanted her for themselves. She didn't want to share her with anybody. So she put her in a tower and sealed up the door behind her, and at the end of every day she brought food for her. There was no way into the tower now of course, so what happened was this: the witch would call out,

> *"Rapunzel, Rapunzel,*
> *let down your hair."*

Then Rapunzel would lean out of her window at the top of the tower and wind her hair round two hooks and lower it, and down it would flow, down and down like a shimmering golden waterfall all the way to the ground. The witch would tuck up her skirts and shin up Rapunzel's hair as if it was a ladder, and when she wanted to go home to bed she would swing back down again.

There wasn't much for Rapunzel to do, shut up there in her high tower, except to dream and sing. She had a lovely voice, and one day a young prince was riding through the forest and he heard her voice and fell in love with it. He had to know who it belonged to. He found the tower but there was no door to it. He walked round and round, looking up hopelessly at its high, smooth walls. Nobody could be in there, surely, he thought,

and yet there was the voice, as sweet as a skylark. He was just about to ride away, sure now that he must be imagining it, when he saw the witch coming through the forest towards the tower, and he hid among the bushes.

*"Rapunzel, Rapunzel,*
*let down your hair,"*

he heard her say. The singing stopped and down came the curtain of glorious hair, and up the witch climbed. Now he had no doubt that somebody was hidden in the tower, and he couldn't wait to see who it was.

As soon as the witch had climbed down again and disappeared into the forest, the prince approached the tower. It was almost night by now, and he was a little afraid that he might be

under a spell of some sort, he had such longing to
see who was sealed in the tower.

*"Rapunzel, Rapunzel,*
*let down your hair,"*

he called, and sure enough the shower of hair
came flowing down. The prince swung himself
up. Imagine his surprise when he found himself
facing a young girl who was so beautiful in the
moonlight that she stole his heart away. And
imagine her surprise, when she was expecting
a green-eyed spiky witch, to see a young man
smiling at her.

Rapunzel had never seen a man before. She had
no idea what a prince was. She had never heard of
love. But she was very happy. The prince stayed
with her until a dawn like pearls was creeping

across the sky, and when he left her she knew that she couldn't live without him.

He came the next night, and the next, and the next, and when he asked her if she would be his wife she said *yes*, even though she had no idea what a wife was.

"But this is no good, you know," he said. "I have a fine palace just over the hill. That's where we should be."

So they thought up a wonderful plan for Rapunzel's escape. Every time the prince came to see her he brought her some silk, and all day long when she was without him she wove a ladder for herself. It gave her something to do while she was singing, and each rung she wove brought her a step nearer to freedom.

And all would have been well if she hadn't

forgotten herself completely one day. This is what happened. The witch climbed up at dusk, as usual, and Rapunzel said carelessly, "I always know when it's you coming. You're so much heavier than..." She went pale and put her hand to her mouth, but the witch slapped it away, quick as a fly.

"Heavier than what? Heavier than who?"

"Than the prince who comes to see me," Rapunzel confessed.

"You wicked girl! You've deceived me!" In a rage that was as wild as a thunderstorm the witch pulled back Rapunzel's wonderful hair and cut it off – snip! She forced her down the silk ladder that would have taken her into the prince's arms, and sent her out into the wilderness to live or to die, she no longer cared which.

That night the prince came to take Rapunzel home with him.

*"Rapunzel, Rapunzel,*
*let down your hair,"*

he called, and this time the silk ladder came down. Up he climbed, but when he reached the tower it was not Rapunzel's eyes that he looked into, but the deep bog-pond green of the witch's.

"Ha! Your bird has flown away!" she cackled. "So fly after her!" She cut the silk ladder – snip! and down he tumbled, down and down, and would have broken his neck if he hadn't been saved by a briar bush. But the thorns pierced his eyes and blinded him, and with the witch's

laughter ringing in his ears the prince wandered away into a darkness that was deeper than night itself.

He wandered for many days and many weeks and many months, eating nuts and berries that he found on the wayside, and a year and a day later he came into the same part of the wilderness as Rapunzel. She recognized him at once and ran to him and put her arms round him, and her tears washed his eyes and he could see again.

He took her home to his palace, and they announced their wedding, and the prince and his Rapunzel lived happily ever after.

And as for the witch – well, as far as I know, she's still trapped in the tower.

# SNOW WHITE

On a winter's day, long, long ago, a queen was sitting by her window sewing. Outside the snow was drifting down like the feathers of a swan and settling on the black branches of the trees. The queen pricked her finger and three drops of blood like crimson tears trickled on to the snow, and the queen thought, "How I would love to have a daughter who was as white as the snow, and as black as the branches, and as red as blood. How beautiful she would be. And I would call her Snow White."

But when her child was born, the queen died. After a time the king married again. The new queen was very vain. She had a mirror which she would gaze into every day, and the mirror always showed her how beautiful she was. And one day she asked it out loud:

*"Mirror, mirror in my hand,*
*    Who is the fairest in the land?"*

And the mirror said:

*"You are lovely, it is true,*
*    But Snow White is far lovelier than you."*

"What!" The queen threw the mirror on to her bed and ran to Snow White's room.

The child was by now seven years old. Her hair was as black as winter branches, and her skin

was as white as snow, and her lips were as red as blood. It was true. She was beautiful, so beautiful that the queen couldn't bear to look at her.

"Take her away!" the queen shouted to the castle huntsman. "Take her into the woods. Kill her! And bring me her heart, so I know she's truly dead."

But when they were deep in the forest the huntsman took pity on the child and knew that he couldn't do what the queen had asked him to do. He slipped away from Snow White and left her, with the wild creatures of the forest prowling round. But he daren't go back to the castle empty-handed, so he killed one of the wild boars and took its heart to the queen and gave it to her, and she cooked it and ate it.

Snow White was afraid. She wandered

through the forest, stumbling over the twisted roots of trees and the sharp stones, and at last she saw a cottage and ran to the door. There was no reply to her knock. The door was unlocked and she went in, and there she found a fire ready for lighting, and a table with seven places set for eating, and chairs ready to be sat on. There were seven chairs and she tried them all, every one, and one was too hard and one was too soft, one too creaky and one too slippy, one too high and one too low; and one just right. And every chair she sat on was placed in front of a bowl of food, and she had a spoonful out of every one of them, and felt much better.

She climbed upstairs and looked into the bedroom and there she found seven beds that were ready for sleeping in, and she tried them all.

One was too hard and one was too soft, one too creaky and one too slippy, and one too high and one too low; and one just right, and when she tried that one she fell at once into a deep, peaceful sleep.

When dusk came the owners of the cottage came home for their supper. They had been toiling in the mines all day and were tired and hungry.

But, "What's this?" one of them said. "Someone's been sitting in my chair and nibbling at my supper."

"And mine!"

"And mine!" the others all called out.

They ate what was left of their food, grumbling to each other, and then they trudged upstairs, ready to tumble into bed.

But, "What's this?" one of them said. "Someone's been in my bed!"

"And mine!"

"And mine!" the others all called out.

And the seventh one said, "There's someone *in* my bed! Look at her. Don't wake her up! Look how beautiful she is."

The others all crowded round the bed and gazed down in silence at Snow White, and then they tiptoed back to their own beds and let the seventh share with each of them in turn, so that the little girl wouldn't be disturbed.

Next morning Snow White woke up to find the seven miners all ready for work and having their breakfast. They were dwarfs, and no bigger than she was, but she was afraid because she had eaten their food and slept in their beds.

"What's this?" one of them said. "No

need to be scared of us, child. But tell us why you're here."

So she told them the whole story of the queen and how she had made the huntsman take her into the forest to kill her. The dwarfs muttered and rumbled and pulled their beards and then said that she mustn't go back to the castle, ever. She could stay and make her home with them, and in return she could keep it clean and tidy and cook their meals and wash their clothes and sew for them. Snow White had never done anything like that before because she was a princess. She found that she loved doing it because the dwarfs were so kind to her, and she was very happy.

The queen was very happy too, now she'd got rid of her stepdaughter. But one day she picked up her mirror and learnt the truth.

*"Mirror, mirror in my hand,*
*Who is the fairest in the land?"*

And the mirror said:

*"You are lovely, it is true,*
*But Snow White is far lovelier than you."*

"What! Still living?" In a rage the queen sent for the huntsman and had him beheaded, and then she dressed herself in his clothes and searched through the forest for Snow White. At last she came to a cottage with smoke curling from the

chimney. She peered through the window and saw Snow White setting the table for supper, and she smiled to herself and knocked on the glass.

"Snow White! I've come to see how you are," she said. "Let me in."

Now Snow White had promised the seven dwarfs that she would never let anyone into the cottage. But it was only the huntsman. She went to the window and smiled at him.

"I've brought you a present!" the queen said, dangling a lacy shawl. "Look! As white as your skin! Won't you let me fasten it round your shoulders?"

Snow White opened the door, and before she had time to realize that the visitor wasn't the huntsman at all, the queen had wrapped the shawl round her shoulders and pulled it so tight across her chest that it took her breath away. She fell to the floor and lay as still as death.

"You can say goodbye to your beauty now!" the queen said.

When dusk came down and the dwarfs came home they were horrified to find Snow White lying on the ground.

"What's this!" one of them said. "She's dead! Snow White is dead!" But when they loosened her shawl she breathed again and sat up.

"You can be quite sure it was the queen who did this," they told her. "Never, never let anyone in again."

"I promise," Snow White said.

Well, the queen was triumphant. Next day she picked up her mirror and smiled into it.

*"Mirror, mirror in my hand,*
*Who is the fairest in the land?"*

And the mirror replied:

*"You are lovely, it is true,*
*But Snow White is far lovelier than you."*

"What!" Now the queen's fury was a terrible thing to see. She whirled through the castle like a wild wind, taking this and taking that, and at last she emerged dressed like a pedlar and carrying a tray of trinkets – sky-blue ribbons and silky bows and the prettiest pearl comb, which she had dipped in poison. She came to the cottage and looked through the window. Snow White was sewing by the fire. The queen tapped on the glass and said, "Ribbons for sale!"

"No thank you," called Snow White.

"Pretty bows for your dress."

"No."

"A comb for your lovely black hair. Come and look, dear."

Well, there was no harm in looking. When Snow White saw that it was only a poor pedlar she opened the window. The queen picked up the comb and held it out and smiled.

"Here you are, dear."

Snow White lifted it to her hair. But it was so full of poison that as soon as it touched her head Snow White gave a gasp of pain and fell to the ground. And there

she lay, as still and white as death.

"Farewell, little beauty," said the queen.

At dusk, when the dwarfs came home, they found Snow White stretched out. "What's this! She's dead!" But they saw the comb in her hair and as soon as they lifted it out she opened her eyes and sat up again.

"It was the queen, the queen," they told her. "Never, never open the door or the window to anyone, Snow White."

And she promised that she wouldn't.

In the palace the queen laughed with joy. "Now I'm the most beautiful person in the world!" She had to be.

Next morning she picked up the mirror playfully and sang to it:

*"Mirror, mirror in my hand,*
*Who is the fairest in the land?"*

And the mirror said:

*"You are lovely, it is true,*
*But Snow White is far lovelier than you."*

"What?" The queen gazed at her reflection, and saw a face that was ugly with hatred. She hurled the mirror on to the bed. She sent for a farmer's wife and threw her into a cell and took her clothes. She picked an apple, red on one side, green on the other, and she poisoned the red side. Then she set out again for the cottage of the seven dwarfs.

"Open up, dear," she called, tapping on the window.

"No, I can't let you in," Snow White said.

But it was only a simple farmer's wife, after all. Snow White opened the window a crack.

"Would you like a bite of my apple?" the queen said, smiling.

"No thank you."

But it did look juicy and sweet.

The queen took a bite from the green side herself and held the apple out to Snow White. "It's just for you. As red as your lips," she said. "Taste it!"

Snow White bit the apple, and fell down dead.

When the dwarfs returned at

dusk she was lying cold and still on the ground. They crouched down and listened for her breath, and looked at each other with grief in their eyes. "She is dead. Snow White is truly dead."

They couldn't bear the thought of never seeing her again. So they made a coffin of glass, and gently laid her in it, and carried it to the hill behind the house. Every day one of the dwarfs visited her and put new flowers by her. A raven came to see her, its wings as black as her hair. A robin came to see her, its breast as red as her lips. A dove came to see her, as white as her skin.

And seven years later, a prince came. He climbed up the hill, curious to see what was in the glass box up there, and

when he saw Snow White he fell in love with her. He begged the dwarfs to let him take her to his palace, where he might look at her all day, but they refused.

"We'd be lost without her," they said. "We'd miss her too much."

But they were moved by his love for her. He came every day, and they muttered and rumbled and pulled their beards and one of them said, "This is such a rough and humble place for her. And she is royal, after all. A king's daughter. Maybe we should let the prince take her to his palace."

So they agreed, and he was speechless with happiness.

As he lifted the glass coffin the piece of apple fell from Snow White's lips and she

opened her eyes. She gazed in wonder at the prince. He lifted up the lid and held her hand and she stepped out, not a child but a beautiful girl. He asked her to marry him, and she said *yes*.

It was the greatest wedding the country had ever known. Even the wicked queen was invited. That morning, as the bells were ringing out, she looked into her mirror. Every day for seven years the mirror had said to her, "You are the loveliest, it is true." How she loved to hear it. How she loved her mirror. So today she said again:

> *"Mirror, mirror in my hand,*
> *Who is the fairest in the land?"*

But the mirror said:

> *"You are lovely, it is true,*
> *But the bride is lovelier than you."*

"What!" The queen dashed the mirror to the ground, where it smashed into a million glass splinters. She rushed to the prince's palace with horror and disbelief in her heart. But it was true. There was the prince's bride, and it was Snow White.

"Just in time for the dancing!" the dwarfs said to the queen, handing her a pair of shoes. "Dance for the prince's bride!" But the shoes had been filled with red-hot coals, and the wicked queen danced and she danced and she danced until she died.

And as for the
prince and Snow White,
they lived happily ever after.

# ALADDIN AND THE ENCHANTED LAMP

In a city in China long ago, there lived a poor widow and her only son, Aladdin.

One day a sorcerer came looking for something in that very city. He knew what it was he was looking for, but he needed someone very small and quick to get it for him. And when he saw Aladdin dodging round the bazaar and helping himself to fruit off the stalls he knew he had found exactly the right person. He pretended to be his long-lost uncle, and promised him a carpet shop if he would help him. Aladdin couldn't believe his luck. Neither could his mother.

"You haven't got an uncle," she told him. "But this man looks as if he's got more money than sense. Bring him in."

So, next day the sorcerer took Aladdin for a walk, and they ended up in a chrysanthemum garden. "Ah, at last!" the sorcerer sighed. "I've come all the way from Morocco to find this garden. Now you can help me."

He asked Aladdin to gather twigs and light a fire, then he threw a pinch of incense into the flames. The sky grew dark and the earth was covered with sweet smoke. And when the smoke cleared, there was a marble slab with a golden ring right in front of them. "Lift the slab," the sorcerer said. "Only you can do it."

The slab looked very heavy, and Aladdin's muscles were the size of peas, but he did as he was told, reciting his name and his mother's as he pulled, and up the slab came as if it was made of paper.

"Now," said the sorcerer, clapping his hands, "there are caves full of treasure down there. I want you to go down and walk through four caverns. Each will contain four gold chests. Don't touch them, or anything around them, or you'll be turned into stone. Go through into the fourth chamber and out into a garden of fruit trees, and through that, up some stairs, you will see a lamp hanging. Bring it to me. You may take whatever fruit you like from the trees, but nothing else."

The sorcerer took off his ring and put it on Aladdin's finger. "This will keep you safe. You are a man now."

Fearful and proud and excited, Aladdin did as

he was told. He went down into the dark cave
and into a cavern with walls crusted with green
emeralds, and another crusted with red rubies,
and another with blue amethysts, and another
with shimmering diamonds, so bright that you
would think the stars had fallen out of the sky.

In each of the caverns there were chests over-
flowing with gold coins, but Aladdin hurried
past them all, and came into a garden where the
trees were loaded down with glowing fruit. He
hurried past, and climbed up the steps at the
end, and there he found the lamp. There was
nothing special about it, in fact it was battered
and rusty, but he tucked it under his shirt.

When he came to the fruit he remembered that
he could take some, but as soon as he touched
them the apples and lemons and pineapples and

cherries all turned into glass, every one. The colours were so rich and beautiful that he wanted to show them to his mother and he took them anyway, and stuffed them into his pockets and down his shirt and up his sleeves. He could hardly move, and when he reached the way out he couldn't climb up to it.

"Uncle, give me a hand," he called up.

"Pass the lamp up, pass the lamp up," the sorcerer hissed.

"I can't! I'm stuck! Help me out first."

Well, the sorcerer was sure that Aladdin was trying to steal the lamp from him.

"Once a thief, always a thief!" he snarled. In a rage he slammed the slab back over Aladdin's head and sealed him underground.

Aladdin didn't know what to do with himself.

He wrung his hands in despair, and by chance he rubbed the ring that the sorcerer had given him. At once there was a puff of smoke and a little fat genie appeared, sitting cross-legged about half a metre off the ground, arms folded and smiling like a cat.

"I am the genie of the ring. Tell me your wish, O Master."

"Get me out of here!" No sooner had Aladdin said it than he was back in the bazaar telling his mother about the wonderful things he had seen in the caverns. She didn't believe a word of it.

"So much fuss over a rusty old lamp," she said. "Well, the best thing I can do is sell it! Not that we'll get much for it. I'll just give it a bit of a polish and see if I can brighten it up." She rubbed it with an old cloth and *flash!* another genie appeared, pouring himself like wreaths of smoke out of the mouth of the lamp, rising higher and higher above them until he was taller than a temple. Aladdin's mother fell to her knees in fright, but by now Aladdin knew what genies could do.

"What is your wish, O Master?" the genie asked, in a voice that rumbled like the heart of a volcano.

"Slave of the lamp," Aladdin said, as if he was the sultan himself, "fetch us some food."

*Puff!* The genie disappeared. A flash or two later he was back with a silver tray loaded with so many plates of food that Aladdin and his mother didn't stop eating for a month. Then Aladdin sold the silver plates and, after that, the tray, and he and his mother were better off than they had ever been in their lives.

But then, something even more wonderful happened to Aladdin. He fell in love. It was quite easy to see that this had happened because he stopped eating or sleeping and mooned round the bazaar singing and sighing until at last his mother said, "Tell me who she is, Aladdin. This girl who's stolen your heart away. Who is she?"

"The sultan's daughter," he said gloomily. "The beautiful Princess Badr-al-Budur! I thought all women looked like you, Mother, but now I've seen her I know what real beauty is."

"Well!" gasped his mother. "What a thing to say!"

"I want to marry her, Mother."

"Marry the sultan's daughter! Are you mad! He'll have your head for a cannon ball if you ask him to give you his daughter."

"That's why I want you to ask him for me," Aladdin said. "But what gifts can I send?"

And then he remembered the glass fruits that

he had brought from the cave. As he unwrapped them they saw them for what they really were – not glass at all, but rubies and diamonds, topaz, emeralds, amethyst, all glittering and sparkling and flashing like fishes in a stream.

"Take these to the sultan," Aladdin begged his mother. "And ask if I can marry the Princess Badr-al-Budur."

And his mother did. She had to go to the golden palace every day for a week, and queue up with all the other people who had brought gifts, but at last the sultan agreed to see her. He was so impressed with her wealth that he agreed that his daughter would marry Aladdin in three months' time. Aladdin's mother rushed home and danced all round the bazaar with her son.

But the sultan didn't keep his word. A month

later the Princess Badr-al-Budur was married to the son of the sultan's grand-vizier. Aladdin was mad with despair. He snatched up his enchanted lamp and rubbed it and *flash!* up billowed the genie in a cloud of green smoke.

"What is your wish, O Master?" he rumbled, bowing to the ground.

"Bring me the princess and that soppy-faced husband of hers!" Aladdin ordered, and it was done. No sooner had the princess and the son of the grand-vizier climbed into bed for the night than the bed whizzed out of the window and over the town and landed in Aladdin's house. He threw the grand-vizier's son out on to the dung heap. This happened night after night, until at last the princess and the grand-vizier's son were so fed up with this treatment that they decided the marriage was definitely off. And next day, Aladdin's mother was knocking at the palace door demanding to see the sultan.

"You promised the princess to my son," she reminded him.

"Ah, so I did," said the sultan. "Well, it looks as if she isn't married after all. Tell your son that if he can bring me forty times the jewels he brought before, with forty slaves and forty slave-girls to carry them, he can marry my daughter."

Aladdin's mother trudged home with the news. "I wish you'd never clapped eyes on that princess," she said. "Where are you going to get that lot from, Aladdin?"

He picked up his enchanted lamp and rubbed it, and *flash!* up flowed the genie, bowing low.

"What is your wish, O Master?"

Before Aladdin's mother had time to tidy up the house, it was full of slaves and slave-girls staggering under the weight of their trays of jewels. She led them off to the palace at once, and this time the sultan welcomed her with open arms. She ran home to Aladdin, and they danced round the bazaar and all the way up to the palace, with more slaves and jewels sent up by the helpful genie. The sultan himself came out to meet them and flung his arms round Aladdin.

"What a splendid son-in-law you'll make! Of course you can marry my daughter! Why didn't you ask me before?"

But Aladdin had a request to make. "I can't marry your daughter until I have built a beautiful palace for her," he said. "May I have this plot of land just in front of yours?"

"Of course. But won't it take a little time?"

"Leave it to me," said Aladdin. When he got home he rubbed his enchanted lamp and called up the genie, and during the night the most exquisite palace sprang up, as golden as the sun itself and glittering with jewels that were every colour of the rainbow. The sultan's palace looked quite small behind it.

"Wonderful!" breathed the sultan, gazing at it out of his window. "How on earth did he do it?"

"By magic," his grand-vizier said. "Only magic could do this. Believe me."

So the Princess Badr-al-Budur and Aladdin were married at last, and they moved into the shimmering palace with Aladdin's mother, and were very happy.

But that isn't the end of the story.

Far away in Morocco the sorcerer heard about the wonderful palace that had sprung up as if by magic, and he came to China to look at it. As soon as he knew that Aladdin was living in it he guessed what had happened. He disguised himself as an old man and had some lamps made, and went round the streets calling out the strangest thing: "New lamps for old! New lamps for old!" Everyone thought he was mad. The princess heard him and sent her maid to fetch him in.

"Give him that rusty old lamp of Aladdin's!" she said. "I'll surprise him with a nice new one."

But there was no time for that. As soon as the maid came out with the lamp, the sorcerer snatched it out of her hands and rubbed it. *Flash!* the genie appeared. "What is your wish, O Master?"

"Take me and this palace and the princess to

Morocco right away."

And it was no sooner said than done. The palace and the princess disappeared as if they had never been, and the sultan was furious. He sent his guards out to find Aladdin and flung him and his mother into prison.

"Now see what you've done," his mother moaned, but the sultan's anger was even greater.

"I've had enough of your magic tricks! Find my daughter, or I'll throw your head on the dung heap. *And* your mother's."

So Aladdin was freed for forty days, but he had no idea what to do or where to look. He went to wash himself in a stream so he could think clearly, and as he wrung his hands together he rubbed his ring. Suddenly, *puff!* a cloud of smoke, and the forgotten fat little genie of the ring appeared.

"What is your wish, O Master?"

Aladdin could have wept for joy. "Take me to my wife," he begged. "That's all I want."

The genie stroked his wispy beard. "I can get you there, but I can't get you back," he said. "It'll use up all my magic as it is."

Aladdin found himself being lifted up and floated over the temples and mountains of China, and over the blue of the oceans, and over the golden deserts of Africa, and at last he was in the arms of his princess.

"Tell me where my lamp is," he asked her, "and we can go back home."

"Your lamp! But I gave it to the maid, and she gave it to the old man. He's the one who brought me here."

Aladdin knew at once who it must be.

The sorcerer was fast asleep, snoring away in Aladdin's own bed. Aladdin crept up to him and stole the lamp from inside his shirt, rubbed it quickly, and *flash!* there was his genie, towering over him and bowing to the ground.

"Take us home!" Aladdin asked him. "O wonderful genie, take us home!"

*Puff!* The palace was returned to China. Aladdin gave the sultan the sorcerer's head instead of his own, the sultan embraced his daughter and his son-in-law, Aladdin's mother was released from prison, and they all lived in great happiness until the day they died.

And that *is* the end of the story.

# LITTLE RED RIDING HOOD

Long ago there was a little girl who lived near the dark woods. Everybody knew her as Little Red Riding Hood because she always wore a velvet red cloak and hood that her grandmother had made for her. One day her mother asked her to put on her cloak and hood and go and visit her grandmother, who was very ill. She put some eggs and butter and a cake in her basket.

"Run along now," she said. "Keep to the path. And don't be long."

The grandmother lived in a cottage at the other side of the woods, and Little Red Riding Hood knew her way there very well. She could have been there and back in no time at all if she hadn't stopped to talk to a wolf on the way.

But she did.

The wolf was watching out for something rabbity to eat, but when he saw the flash of the red cloak he stopped sniffing the grass and lifted his snout in the air. Now he could smell something much tastier than rabbits; a basket full of cake and eggs and butter. He licked his lips and stepped right into the middle of the path, and waited for Little Red Riding Hood.

"Mmm, where are you going with that basket

full of good things to eat?" he asked her, making his voice as charming and gentle as he could.

"I'm going to my grandmother's," said Little Red Riding Hood. She knew she wasn't supposed to talk to wolves but he was polite and softly spoken and besides, he had spoken to her first. "She's not well," she added, to be friendly.

"I'm sorry to hear that," said the wolf, sniffing at the cake. "Perhaps I'll call on her myself. Where does she live?"

"On the other side of these woods," said Little Red Riding Hood, "just by the nut trees."

"Perhaps I could carry your basket for you?" offered the wolf. He could run off with it, he thought, and guzzle up the cake in no time. It made his snout tickle just to think about it. But then he heard the whistle of the huntsman and he decided to keep out of sight. Also, he had thought of something much tastier than butter and cake for his tea.

"Now, why don't you fill your basket up with bluebells for your grandmother? Step into the woods and you'll see them, my dear. What could be a nicer present?"

"That's a good idea. Thank you, Mr Wolf." Little Red Riding Hood stepped off the path and went deeper and deeper into the shadowy woods, where even the birds had stopped singing.

Straight away the wolf ran like the river to the grandmother's cottage, sniggering to himself all the way. He knocked on the door, tappity tap-tap-tap, and he heard the old lady call out, "Who is it?"

"It's Little Red Riding Hood, Grandmother," he said, as light and sweet as he could.

"Oh, lovely! I can't come to the door, my dear,

because I'm in bed. Lift up the latch and come right in."

And in went Mr Wolf with his long wet tongue and his sharp yellow teeth and his eyes as bright as knives and forks, and he gobbled her up in one quick gulp.

But a little skinny grandmother isn't enough to keep a hungry wolf happy. He could think of something even tastier to eat. He climbed into her bed and put on her night-cap and pulled the curtains around himself, and waited for Little Red Riding Hood to come along.

And at last she came, with her basket brimming with bluebells. She knocked on the door of the cottage. Tappity tap-tap-tap.

"Who is it?" came a voice from inside.

"It's Little Red Riding Hood, Grandmother!"

"Oh, lovely! I can't come to the door, my dear, because I'm in bed. Lift up the latch and come right in," said the wolf, as soft and weak as he could.

So Little Red Riding Hood lifted the latch and opened the door.

It was all dark in Grandmother's house, and quiet and still and waiting. She put down her basket by the door and stood with her hands clasped together.

"Where are you, Grandmother?" she whispered.

There was no answer but the sound of snoring from the grandmother's bed. Little Red Riding Hood went up to it and stood very still.

"What loud snores you have, Grandmother," she said.

"All the better to dream of you, my dear. Open the curtains."

Slowly she pulled back the curtains round the bed. She could see her grandmother's head on the pillow, with her night-cap pulled around her face.

"Oh, Grandmother, what big ears you have!"

"All the better to hear you with, my dear. Come a bit closer."

"Oh, Grandmother, what big eyes you have!"

"All the better to see you with, my dear. Come closer."

"But Grandmother, what big hands you have!"

"All the better to hug you with, my dear. Closer."

"But Grandmother! What big teeth you have!"

"All the better to eat you with, my dear." And with that the wolf grabbed hold of Little Red Riding Hood and gobbled her up.

Now, the huntsman who had been in the woods happened to be passing the grandmother's cottage, and he saw that the door was standing open and heard terrible loud snores coming from inside. He went a little nearer, and he saw Little Red Riding Hood's basket standing by the threshold, full of bluebells and cake and butter. He went a little nearer, and he saw the wolf fast asleep on the grandmother's bed.

## LITTLE RED RIDING HOOD

"Ha ha! Old sinner. Caught you at last, have I!" He would have shot him at that very minute, but he saw that the wolf was wearing the grandmother's night-cap. "Gobbled her up, have you? Let's have a look."

He took a pair of scissors and went snippety snip-snip across the wolf's tummy, and saw something velvety red inside. Snippety snip-snip, and out tumbled Little Red Riding Hood. "It was so dark in there!" Little Red Riding Hood said. And out stumbled her grandmother, blinking in the light and glad to be alive.

"Let's give the old wolf some proper food!" Little Red Riding Hood ran outside and collected stones, and put them inside the wolf's belly. She and her grandmother sewed him up, good and tight. "Wake up, Mr Wolf!" she said then.

When he woke up and saw the huntsman and the grandmother and Little Red Riding Hood all standing round him the wolf jumped out of bed in fright and tried to run away, but the stones were so heavy that he fell down dead.

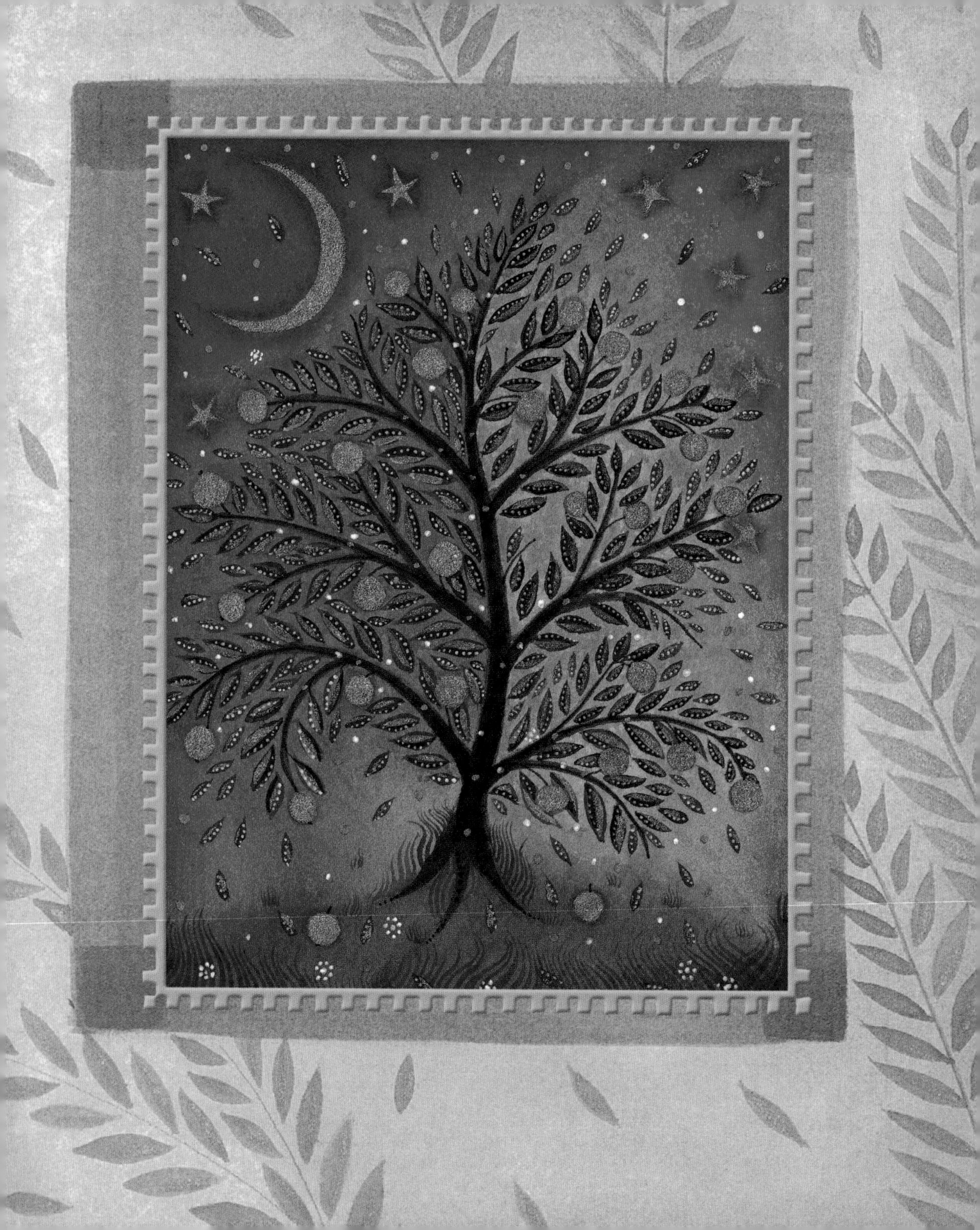

# THE FIRE-BIRD

A long time ago in Russia there was a tsar whose name was Bendei. He had three sons, and the youngest was called Ivan. In the garden of the tsar's palace there was a wonderful tree that bore golden apples. The tsar loved it more than any of his other possessions. One day he discovered that someone was stealing the apples from his tree. Of course, he was heart-broken, and he became ill.

He couldn't eat or drink because his precious golden apples were being stolen. He asked his oldest son to sit by the tree all night and keep watch, but the son fell asleep. He told his father that nobody had come to the garden, but it was quite clear that another apple had been stolen. So the tsar asked his second son to keep watch, and *he* fell asleep. Next day he told his father that no one had come to the garden, but when they counted the apples it was quite clear that yet another one had been stolen.

The tsar was beside himself with worry, so he asked his youngest son, Ivan, to keep watch in the garden. The night was long and warm and Ivan nearly fell asleep too, but he washed his face with dew to keep himself awake. And then he saw an amazing sight that took his breath away.

# THE FIRE-BIRD

Something was glowing like fire in the heart of the tree, and when Ivan ran to it, he saw that it was a beautiful bird, with feathers of red and orange and yellow and gold, just like flames; and that it was busily pecking away at the apples. Ivan ran to catch it but the bird slipped out of his fingers and rose up into the night sky like a fiery comet, and all that was left was one of its golden tail feathers.

"I would love to have that bird," the tsar said next morning, when Ivan showed him the feather. "I think I would love it more than I love my apple tree."

So the three sons set off to find it for him. But the first son was so lazy that he fell asleep as soon as they were outside the walls of the palace; and the second son wasn't much better. He fell asleep under the first tree he came to. And that left Ivan, trotting along on his little white pony and quite happy to be out in the sunshine. But there was no sign of the beautiful bird anywhere.

After a while Ivan stopped, hobbled his pony with a sash so it wouldn't wander away, and went to find something to eat. Along came a big grey wolf and his eyes opened wide at the sight of the pony standing all by itself, and without thinking twice about it he gobbled it up for his dinner. When Ivan came back with some bread and cheese, all that was left of his pony was a heap of bones under the tree. He couldn't believe it.

"My poor pony!" he gasped. "Now what am I going to do? I'm a long, long way from home, and I still haven't found the fire-bird."

The grey wolf was licking his chops under a tree, but when he heard Ivan crying he loped over to him.

"I'm sorry I ate your pony," he said. "But I was hungry. I owe you a favour."

"What use are you to me?" Ivan said.

"I happen to be the only one who knows where the fire-bird lives. Climb on my back and I'll take you there. I promise you will have it for your father."

So Ivan climbed on to the wolf's back and clung on to his thick grey fur, and they sped like the wind itself past shining lakes and through dark forests and over rocky mountains until they came to a castle. And there the wolf stopped.

"Listen carefully to every word I say," he told Ivan. "Go past the sleeping guards. You will see a tower with a golden cage, and inside it, the fire-bird."

"Thank you!" said Ivan.

"Wait," the wolf said. "I haven't finished. You must not touch the cage. Remember that."

So Ivan crept past the snoring guards and up the creaking stairs of the tower to the room at the very top. There in the window was the fire-bird shining like the sun in its golden cage, and the door of the cage was open. Very carefully Ivan lifted the bird out.

"Oh, but it's a beautiful cage," he thought, and touched it, and as he did so the bars chimed out like bells. Everybody in the castle woke up at once, shouting to each other that there was a thief in the tower. Ivan was seized and bundled into the chamber of Tsar Afron himself.

"Who are you, to come creeping into my castle and steal my fire-bird?" the tsar roared. "You deserve to be put to death."

# THE FIRE-BIRD

Ivan went down on his knees. "For the sake of my old father, Tsar Bendei, please forgive me," he begged. "I only did it because he loved your fire-bird so much and wanted to see it for himself."

"The son of a tsar, a common thief! This is worse than I thought!" But Tsar Afron was cunning, and he knew that if Ivan had managed to find his fire-bird then he must be very clever.

"I'll give you one chance," he said. "Somewhere across the purple mountains is the castle of Tsar Kusman. He has a horse with a golden mane. How I would love that horse! Bring it to me, and you can have your fire-bird!"

So Ivan went back to the wolf, and the wolf growled, "Why didn't you listen to me! But a promise is a promise." And he took Ivan on his back over the purple mountains to the castle of Tsar Kusman.

"Listen carefully to every word I say," the wolf said when he set Ivan down. "You will find the horse you are looking for in the stables at the back of the castle."

"Thank you," said Ivan.

"Wait, I haven't finished yet, and you must listen. You will see a golden bridle hanging by the horse. Whatever you do, you must not touch it."

Ivan crept round to the back of the castle and into the stables, and there he found the magnificent horse with the golden mane. He drew the horse away, and just as he was leaving the stable he saw the golden bridle hanging by the door. "Oh, but it's a beautiful bridle," he said, and put out his hand, but as soon as he touched it the bridle jangled and clattered and everyone in the castle woke up. Ivan was seized by the guards and thrown into the spidery dungeon, and the Tsar Kusman came to see him.

"Chop off his head!" he bellowed.

"In the name of my father, Tsar Bendei, please forgive me," Ivan begged.

"How disgraceful! The son of a tsar, a common thief!" Tsar Kusman said. Yet his eyes gleamed, because he knew that Ivan must be very clever indeed to have found the horse with the golden mane. "I will give you one chance," he said. "Find the castle of Tsar Dalmat. I want his dark-eyed

daughter, Ylena the Fair. Bring her to me, and you can have your horse with the golden mane. How's that!" So Ivan went back to the wolf.

"Very well, a promise is a promise. We'll find the castle of Tsar Dalmat. Only I know where it is. But this time, I'll do the stealing myself." He ran to the lake and plunged into the deep, silvery water, and when he came back to shore he had a beautiful princess on his back. "Climb on," he told Ivan, and he sped back over the purple mountains to the castle of Tsar Kusman. "Now take Ylena and exchange her for the horse with the golden mane," he said.

"I can't!" whispered Ivan. "I've fallen in love with her. How can I give her to that horrible tsar!"

"Goodness me!" sighed the wolf. "Well, never mind, a promise is a promise. Hide her, and come with me." He did a somersault in the air, *wheesh!* and as quick as a flash turned into a dark-eyed girl who looked exactly like Ylena the Fair. He and Ivan hurried into the castle.

"Here you are, I've brought Ylena the Fair!" Ivan called, and the tsar was so astonished and pleased to see the beautiful dark-eyed Princess Ylena that he gave Ivan the horse with the golden mane and the bridle as well. Ivan galloped to the tree where the real Ylena was hiding and she climbed up behind him.

"How lucky I am," said Ivan, "to have you and the golden horse!"

In the castle, Tsar Kusman put his hairy arms round the other Ylena. "Will you marry me?" he murmured, and fainted with fright when she did a quick somersault *wheesh!* and turned back into the grey wolf with dripping fangs and yellow hungry eyes. In no time at all the wolf was running alongside Ivan and Ylena to the castle of the Tsar Afron.

"What a shame to part with this horse," Ivan said. "If you remember, wolf, I don't have another one. How can I take Ylena home with me if I don't have a horse to ride?"

The wolf sighed. "Very well," he said. "A promise is a promise. Hide the horse and Ylena in the forest, and come with me." He turned a somersault *wheesh!* as quick as a flash and became a horse with a golden mane, and Ivan climbed on to his back and rode into the castle yard. The Tsar Afron came running out to meet him, rubbing his hands with glee.

"Your father must be so proud to have such a clever son," he said. "Here, the fire-bird is yours, and the golden cage as well."

Ivan left the castle and hurried back to the forest where Ylena was waiting for him with the real horse, and they set off through the night with the glow from the fire-bird lighting their way. And in the yard of the castle the Tsar Afron climbed on to the back of his new horse.

"What a magnificent sight I am!" he roared. "Look at me, everybody!" And he tumbled to the ground in a heap of shouts and bruises when the horse somersaulted *wheesh!* and turned into the grey wolf.

"Now I have kept my promise," the wolf said. "That is the end of it. Goodbye to Ivan, son of Tsar Bendei. He has made his fortune."

Ivan and Ylena galloped for many days before they came near the palace of the Tsar Bendei. "I think we should rest before we go any further," Ivan said. They stopped under a tree and fell asleep in each other's arms.

Not far away, the old tsar lay dying in his bed, grieving for the loss of his youngest son. "He must be dead," he kept saying to his other sons. "And it's all my fault. See if you can find out any news of him at all."

The two brothers set off, and before long they came across their brother, asleep in the arms of a beautiful princess, with a horse with a golden mane grazing near by, and hanging from a branch, the fire-bird in a golden cage. They whistled softly to each other in amazement.

"I'll have the bride, you have the horse, and we'll give Father the fire-bird," the oldest one said.

"And Ivan will know nothing about it. Father thinks he's dead anyway!" said the other. They drew their swords and killed Ivan without even thinking twice, and made off at once with their prizes.

It just happened that the old grey wolf was running past the tree when he saw Ivan lying dead and a raven circling over him.

"I might have known I hadn't seen the last of Ivan," the wolf said. As soon as the raven landed to peck at Ivan the wolf caught her in his fangs. "I will eat your children," he said, "if you don't fly away at once and fetch me the water of life and death."

The raven soared up into the air at once, away over the trees and the mountains, the forests and lakes, and when she came back she had the water of life and death in her beak. "Your children are safe," the wolf said. He bathed Ivan's wounds with some of the drops of water, and they were healed. Then he put the rest of the drops on to Ivan's lips, and Ivan opened his eyes and took

a breath and came back to life. "Now I have done with you," said the wolf, and turned a somersault and disappeared.

Ivan hurried to the palace, and was relieved to find his father still alive. He and Ylena told the old man the true story, and the tsar rose from his death-bed and banished the older brothers from the kingdom, without horse to ride or food to eat, and they were never seen again.

Ivan asked Ylena if she would marry him, and she said *yes*. The fishes of the lake brought her a gown that was the colour of silver water, and it became her wedding-dress, and Ivan gave her the horse with the golden mane for a wedding present. The fire-bird roosts in the tsar's golden apple tree and sleeps at night in its golden cage, which chimes in the wind like sweet, far-away bells.

# HANSEL AND GRETEL

It was a long time ago and a long way away. A boy called Hansel and a girl called Gretel lived with their parents in a cottage by the forest. Times were hard – wolves stole the sheep, foxes stole the hen, the potatoes didn't grow. They were nearly starving, and one night when the children were so hungry that they couldn't sleep, they heard their mother saying, "Husband, husband, there's not enough food left for all of us."

"But what can we do?" they heard their father say.

"Husband, husband, it's quite simple. We must take the children into the forest and leave them to fend for themselves."

"I can't do that," he said.

"If we don't, husband, then we'll all die."

Gretel began to cry then, and Hansel put his arms round her. "Don't worry," he said. "I know what to do."

He waited till his parents were asleep and then he crept outside. The moon was full and bright, and the pebbles on the ground shone like stars. He filled his pockets with them.

Next morning they were woken up by their mother shaking them roughly. "Get up, get up. You must come with us to chop wood." She gave them each a slice of bread, but Hansel slipped his into Gretel's pocket, and they all set off together. Every now and again Hansel lingered behind to drop a pebble on the path.

"Come on, come on," his father urged, anxious to get it all over and done with.

"What are you gawping at, stupid boy?" his mother asked.

"I'm just saying goodbye to my little white cat," Hansel said as he dropped another pebble.

"That's not a cat, you fool. How many times must I tell you! It's the sun shining on the chimney pot!"

When they arrived in the middle of the forest the parents told the children to gather twigs and light a fire. "And wait here till we come for you." They went off without saying goodbye.

The children ate their bread and curled up by the fire. They could hear a sound like the chop,

chop, chop of an axe and thought for a long time that it must be their father near by, but it was only a branch knocking against a pole that their mother had set up to trick them. It grew dark and cold, their little fire died out. But when the moon came up, there were the pebbles that Hansel had dropped, shining like bright eyes and guiding them back home.

When they knocked on the door and their mother opened it she couldn't believe what she was seeing. "Husband! Husband! The children have come home!" She scolded them for staying out so long, but their father's heart rose at the sight of his children.

"We will make do on what we have," he told his wife, and she pursed her lips grimly and said, "We'll have to see, husband."

But bad times came again. The earth was cold and bare, men and beasts groaned with hunger. One night the children lay awake and heard their mother saying, "Husband, husband, something's got to be done. Tomorrow we'll take the children to the forest and leave them there."

Gretel cried, and Hansel put his arms round her and said, "Don't worry, Gretel. I'll think of something." When his parents were asleep he crept downstairs. Outside, the white pebbles gleamed in the moonlight, but his mother had locked the door and he couldn't get to them.

Next morning they had to get up early. "Come on, come on," the children's mother called. "We've got to get some wood for our fire." She gave them a much smaller slice of bread than last time. "Keep it in your pocket for later," she told them.

But every now and again as they walked Hansel lingered behind and crumbled little pieces of bread on to the ground to guide the way back home.

"What are you hanging back there for?" his mother called.

"I'm only looking at the little white dove on our rooftop. It's saying goodbye to me."

"Stupid boy, there's no white dove," his mother snapped. "It's our chimney pot, I keep telling you!"

They walked and walked until there was no walking left in their feet. "Have a rest," their mother told them. "Light a fire and sit here until we come back." And she and her husband went off without saying goodbye.

Hansel had crumbled all his slice of bread

away, so they only had Gretel's piece to share between them. Night was falling; it was growing dark, and their little fire went down. The moon came up and the children searched for the trail of breadcrumbs that would lead them back home, but there was nothing left. The birds of the forest had eaten every crumb.

Hansel and Gretel built up their fire again and covered themselves over with leaves, and tried to shut out the howling and creaking night. When morning came they set off for home again, but the more they walked, the more they got lost, and sometimes it seemed that they passed the same tree eleven times in an hour. They wandered for three nights and three days, and nothing looked right. Nothing looked like the way home, and the trees were high and dark,

blocking out the light of day.

"Follow me! Follow me!" they heard a voice calling, and they saw a white bird gleaming like the moon among the branches. They ran after it, and came to a clearing, and there in the middle was a cottage made of gingerbread.

They went right up to it, quite sure that they must be dreaming, but it was true. Hansel pulled a piece of brandy-snap off the gate and gave Gretel some. Gretel picked two lollipops out of the garden and handed one to Hansel. "Mmm! Taste the door – it's like strawberries!" Hansel said. But Gretel was too busy licking the barley sugar windows. They couldn't stop themselves. They pulled great chunks of sweet and sticky ginger-bread out of the wall and stuffed them into their mouths. The more they ate, the more they wanted.

They heard a voice coming from inside, "Who's that nibbling at my house?"

"It's only a little harvest mouse!" they called, and carried on eating. But then the door opened, and out came the oldest woman in the world. They stopped with their hands full and their cheeks bulging, and stared. Her skin shivered and crinkled like dry leaves and her eyes were as red as burning coals. She was a witch on the look-out for children to eat. But she seemed sweet enough at first. "Come right in," she cooed, just like the white bird. "I've been expecting you." They followed her inside the house and there sure enough was a table laid for two with still more food, and upstairs, two beds with clean white sheets.

Hansel and Gretel slept like angels on white clouds that night. But next morning Gretel woke up to find the witch patting Hansel's rosy cheeks as if they were ripe apples. "He'll do nicely," she crooned. "When he's fattened up a bit more."

"What do you mean?" said Gretel, beginning to be afraid.

"You've had your feast – now I want mine," snapped the witch, all her cooey sweetness gone. She yanked Hansel out of bed and pushed him into a cage in the yard before he had time to blink the sleep out of his eyes. "Now get him fed," she yapped at Gretel. "I like nice fat boys for my supper."

From then on all the best food went to Hansel. Gretel got bread crusts and bits of bacon rind and stale cakes. But she didn't mind about that, she was just worried about poor Hansel. He wasn't enjoying his food much either. Every day the witch told him to put his finger out of the cage so she could squeeze it and see how much fatter he was getting. He played a trick on her. He stuck a bit of chicken bone out of the cage instead of his finger, and the witch's eyesight was so bad that she couldn't tell the difference. But she decided at last that she was too hungry to wait any longer.

"Today's the day!" she said, smacking her lips. "Get a fire going, Gretel. I've a tasty stew to cook."

She filled a cauldron with water and started chopping up vegetables, and as she was chopping she cackled a happy song to herself:

*"Carrots and onions in the pot,*
*And a fat little boy when it's good and hot."*

She threw in the vegetables one by one. Gretel began to cry.

"Gretel," the witch called. "I'm going to make some bread to mop up the gravy. Get the bread tray out of the oven for me."

*"Nothing tastes better than little boy stew*
*With slices of little girl bread to chew,"*

she sang in her crackly voice. "Hurry up, Gretel. The bread tray."

Gretel knew what the witch was going to do. She wasn't going to bake bread at all, she was going to bake *her*. She went to the oven with her heart in her boots.

"I can't turn the handle. It's too stiff," she cried.

"What a useless child you are. Bang it with the poker. Like this." And the witch did it for her.

"But I can't see the bread tray. It's too dark in the oven," Gretel cried.

"What a stupid girl you are. Bend down and reach right in. Like this."

And the witch bent down to do it for her, and quick as a flash Gretel shoved her into the oven and slammed the door. And that was the end of the witch. Burnt to a cinder.

Then Gretel ran to Hansel's cage and let him out. They loaded up their pockets with all the pearls and diamonds that the witch had in her cupboards, and ran and ran from the gingerbread house, ran and ran from the dark forest and the tall trees, and at last they came to their own cottage with its white chimneys.

There was their father, grown old and ill with worrying about them. His wife was dead and gone. He wept when he saw the children. "I thought I would never see you again," he said.

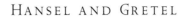

Hansel and Gretel gave him the treasure they had taken from the witch's house, and they all lived in great happiness, and were never hungry again.

# THE FROG PRINCE

On a perfect day a beautiful young princess was playing in her rose garden with a golden ball. It was her favourite toy, and she sang as she threw it high in the air and watched how it gleamed in the sky, just like the sun. She caught it and bounced it, threw it and caught it, bounced it and threw it. All of a sudden it slipped out of her fingers, bounced once, and dropped inside a well.

"My ball!" the princess sobbed. "My lovely golden ball!" She ran to the well and peered in, hoping that she would be able to lean down and pick out the ball, but the water in the well was so deep that she couldn't even see the bottom of it, only the reflection of the sky and her own face looking up at her.

"I'd give anything to have my ball back," the princess said aloud. "I'd give away all my jewels and all my fine silk dresses, if only I could have it back."

As soon as she said that a frog hopped on to the side of the well. He sat dripping just next to the princess's hand, and gazed at her with bulging yellow eyes. "I can help you," he croaked.

"You!" The princess moved her hand away from him quickly. "How can a horrible slimy thing like you do anything to help?"

"I can help get your ball for you, if you promise I can live in your house and eat from your plate and sleep with you in your bed."

"Well, that's not much to promise a silly little frog," the princess laughed, "so I'll say yes!"

And straight away the frog dived into the well, and down and down into the deep dark water, and soon he swam up with the golden ball in his mouth. He rolled it on to the grass and then the princess picked it up and ran home to her castle, bouncing the ball and singing with joy. In the distance she could hear the frog croaking a strange little song, but she tried not to listen to the words.

This is what he sang, as he watched the princess running away from him.

*"Remember the frog and the words that were said,*
*Down by the well where the red roses grow;*
*Your house, and your plate, and your snowy-white bed,*
*For you are my love and my lady-o."*

## THE FROG PRINCE

But the princess sang louder, to drown out his words.

> *"What do I care for your silly song!*
> *You can wait for me all day long,*
> *I'll never go back where the red roses grow*
> *And I'll never be your lady-o."*

That's what she thought.

That night the princess and her father were just sitting down to the table to eat in the lofty hall of their castle when they heard a rat-tat tat, rat tat-a-tat on the great wooden door. The servant opened the door and there on the threshold sat the frog, dripping. The princess put her hand to her mouth and turned her head away quickly. The frog began to sing, and she put her hands over her ears.

*"Remember the frog and the words that were said,*
*Down by the well where the red roses grow;*
*Your house, and your plate, and your snowy-white bed,*
*For you are my love and my lady-o."*

"What does this mean?" her father asked.

So the princess told him how she had lost her favourite golden ball down the well, and how the frog had said he would bring it back to her if she agreed to let him come into her house and eat from her plate and sleep with her in her bed.

"And did you agree?" her father asked.

The princess nodded. "Yes," she whispered, and lowered her head. "But I didn't think he meant it."

And all this time the frog was watching her with his bulging yellow eyes, and gulping and dripping on the threshold.

"Well," her father said. "A promise is a promise. You must ask your frog into the house."

So the princess went to the door and invited the frog to come in, and when she sat down again to her meal he hopped up on to the table beside her, and ate from the side of her plate.

"He is disgusting!" the princess said, but her

father said nothing. When it was time for her to go to bed the princess stood up and the frog hopped a little closer to her and blinked slowly.

"Oh!" she shuddered. "Do I have to take him with me?"

"You made a promise," her father reminded her.

So the princess picked up her candle in one hand and the frog in the other and climbed up the long twisty stairs, to her room. She held the frog well away from her, and in the light of the candle his legs dangled long thin shadows, and his eyes gleamed like deep round wells.

When she woke up the next morning, the frog had gone. "Thank goodness!" the princess said. "Now I can forget all about him."

Next evening, when the princess and her father were just sitting down to their meal there came a rapping at the door, rat-tat-a-tat! and there was the frog, gulping and dripping and slimy, watching her with his bulging yellow eyes.

*"Remember the frog and the words that were said,*
    *Down by the well where the red roses grow;*
*Your house, and your plate, and your snowy-white bed,*
    *For you are my love and my lady-o."*

"A promise is a promise," her father said.

"But he's so disgusting! Oh, he's horrible! Oh, how I hate frogs!"

The princess invited the frog into her house and when she sat down he jumped up and ate from the plate, and when she went to her bed he slept with her on her snow-white sheets. But when morning came, he had gone.

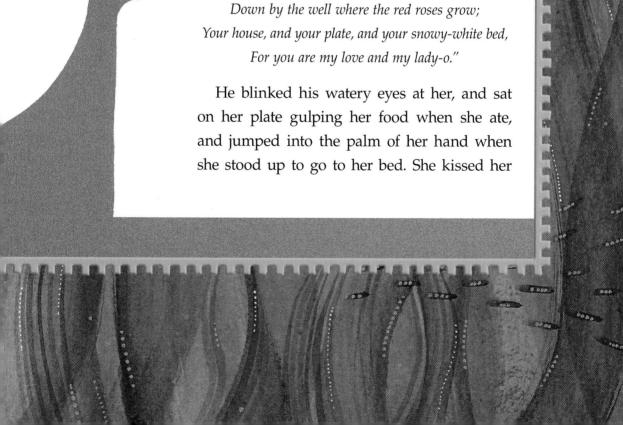

"But he will come tonight, I know it," the princess said. "He'll come every day of my life and I'll never get rid of him."

"That's as may be," said her father. "But a promise is a promise."

And sure enough, the frog came at the end of the day, and sang his song in the doorway.

*"Remember the frog and the words that were said,*
*Down by the well where the red roses grow;*
*Your house, and your plate, and your snowy-white bed,*
*For you are my love and my lady-o."*

He blinked his watery eyes at her, and sat on her plate gulping her food when she ate, and jumped into the palm of her hand when she stood up to go to her bed. She kissed her father goodnight and went sadly up to her room, and put the frog on to her snowy-white pillow, and she sang to him.

*"What do I care for your silly song!*
*You can wait for me all day long,*
*I'll never go back where the red roses grow*
*And I'll never be your lady-o."*

The frog just gazed at her, and gulped, and blinked.

And that night the princess dreamed of the deep dark well, and the red roses that trailed over its mossy walls, and woke up to such a strong scent of roses that she thought for a moment she was in the garden. She lay in her bed half awake and half asleep, watching the sun as it rose in the sky like a golden ball.

"Princess," said a quiet voice, and she sat up startled. Standing by her bed was a young man with bright, smiling eyes.

"Who are you?" the princess asked.

"The frog," he said. "The frog prince."

He took her hand in his and told her that he had been enchanted by a wicked magician who had turned him into a frog and thrown him down the deepest well.

"I watched you every time you came into your garden, and I loved you – but oh! how hopeless it was! You were a princess and I was a frog! But when you let me come into your house and eat from your plate and sleep with you in your bed, you broke the magician's spell. You kept your promise, and that's more powerful than anything a magician can do. You turned me back into a prince."

"I like you much better now you're not a frog," the princess said.

"And I never want to leave you." He took her other hand in his. "I would like to be with you every day of my life, for you are my love and my lady-o."

The princess couldn't help smiling. "Does that mean you want to marry me?" she asked.

"It does," said the frog prince. "Will you?"

And the princess said *yes*.

# THE WILD SWANS

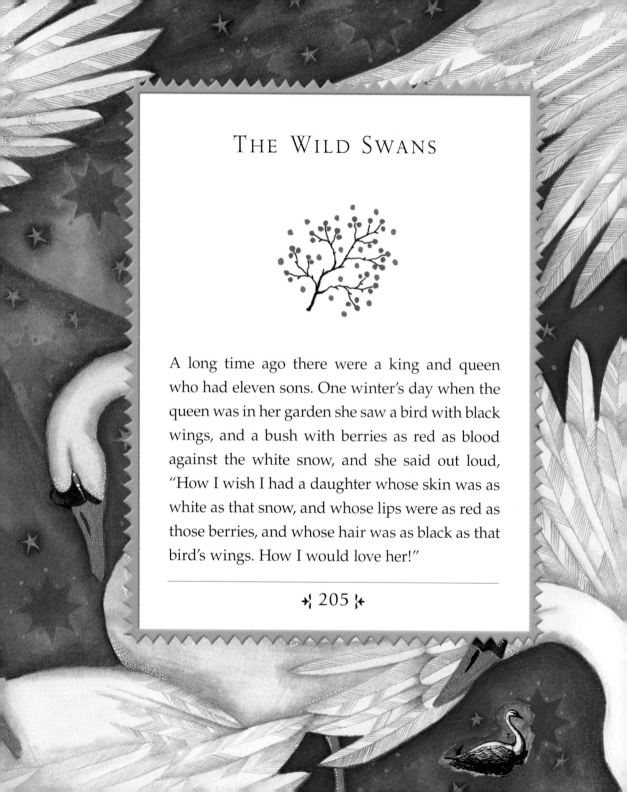

A long time ago there were a king and queen who had eleven sons. One winter's day when the queen was in her garden she saw a bird with black wings, and a bush with berries as red as blood against the white snow, and she said out loud, "How I wish I had a daughter whose skin was as white as that snow, and whose lips were as red as those berries, and whose hair was as black as that bird's wings. How I would love her!"

And instantly an old woman with long grey hair like feathers appeared at her side and said, "That is a foolish wish, but as you have made it, it will be so. You will have the daughter you wish for, but on her twelfth birthday you will lose all your sons."

So the queen had a daughter whose skin was as white as snow, and whose hair was as black as a raven's wing, and whose lips and cheeks were as red as berries. "I name you Snow-rose," the queen said. All her brothers loved her and throughout her childhood they played together in the gardens of the castle. But on the night of Snow-rose's twelfth birthday the queen remembered what the old woman had said.

"We must make our sons safe," she told her husband. "We must lock them inside a tower where no harm can come to them."

## THE WILD SWANS

But there was a window open in the tower, and just as the day was ending there was a sudden rushing and beating of wings and with a strange, sad cry eleven swans flew out into the night and streamed out over the great trees of the castle grounds.

Far below them they could see the castle where their sister was sleeping, and they drifted down towards it, craning their long necks and flapping their great wings.

"Snow-rose!" they called. "Goodbye, Snow-rose."

Snow-rose dreamed about her brothers but didn't know they were there, changed into swans and gliding above her rooftop. When day came they soared up again, high into the air. They flew through many nights and many days until they came to a dark forest stretching down to the sea, and there they landed.

## THE WILD SWANS

When Snow-rose discovered that her brothers had gone, and that she was the cause of it, she begged to be allowed to follow them.

"Ah, no," said the queen. "Don't go. I dread in my heart that I might lose you, too."

But Snow-rose grieved for a year and a day for her lost brothers. And one night when the moon was like a silver boat she let herself out of the castle and ran away to find them.

She wandered for days through the fields and woods, along the whispering rivers, and when she came to the forest it was so dark and deep that she thought she would never see the light of day again. She was hungry and cold and very tired, but when she slept she dreamed that she was with her brothers and that they were playing together in the castle. When she woke

up and saw how dark and huge the forest was, she was more afraid than ever, until glow-worms came to light up the grasses around her, and that brought her some comfort.

In the dim grey morning Snow-rose heard someone coming towards her through the trees. She hid and saw an old woman with hair like feathers, carrying a basket of berries, and begged her to give her some.

"I'm looking for my brothers," she told the woman. "Have you seen eleven princes riding through here?"

"No," the old woman said. "But go down as far as the shore and you will see something that will remind you of your brothers."

So Snow-rose thanked her and went down to the edge of the forest, and there was a wide ocean stretching away from her as far as she could see. She walked along the shore and found eleven swan feathers. She gathered them up, wondering, and as soon as she held them all in her hands she heard a beating of wings and eleven swans circled in the sky above her head, and when darkness was just beginning to fall the swans came down on to the shore and changed into eleven young men, and she recognized them as her brothers.

The girl was filled with joy that she had found them again, but they told her that all through the hours of daylight they had to fly without resting, and by night they changed into young men again, and as soon as day broke they became swans, flying, flying without rest. Her heart was full of pity for them, and she cried because so much suffering had come to them on her account.

"Don't be sad for us," said the youngest brother, her favourite. "We came back hoping to see you, and we have done. But we can't stay any longer than one night on your land. We have our own land now, far away across this sea. We have to go back there at dawn."

"Then take me with you," Snow-rose begged.

So all night without resting they gathered rushes and wove a basket for her, and as soon as day broke and they became swans again the brothers lifted her up into the sky, and the youngest brother flew above her to shield her eyes from the sun.

They flew through all the hours of day, but by dusk they were tiring. Very soon they would turn into young men again. If they didn't find somewhere to land they would fall out of the sky

and drown. At last the youngest brother spied a rock sticking like a seal's head out of the sea, and they landed just in time. The tips of their wing feathers floated away on the dark water. They clung to each other on the tiny rock, too afraid to sleep, and when day came they rose up again, and soared right into the heart of the deepest clouds, where rainbows shone and their reflections glimmered like dazzling ghosts.

They came to land on a beautiful shore near a towering castle. Here they made their home. Even so, Snow-rose only saw her brothers at night. By day they circled the sky or floated over the waves. Snow-rose stood on the shore, gazing after them.

"If only I could help them!" she said out loud, and instantly the old woman appeared at her side.

"If you really mean that, there is a way," the old

woman said. "And you are the only person who can do it."

"What is it? I don't mind how hard it is."

"It is very hard," the old woman assured her. She showed Snow-rose a bunch of stinging nettles that she had in her hand. "These nettles grow all around here. You must gather them with your bare hands, and tread them into flax with your bare feet, and then weave them into eleven coats of mail, each for one of your brothers. Can you bear to do that?"

"Yes, I can," Snow-rose said at once.

"And during all this time you must never say a word," said the old woman, turning away. "Or cry, or sing, or laugh. If you do any of these things, your brothers will be wild swans until the day they die." And with that she was gone.

Straight away Snow-rose ran round the fields gathering nettles with her bare hands. When her brothers returned that night they were distressed to see her sitting by candlelight with great red weals and blisters across her hands and her feet, and with not a word to say to any of them.

"Snow-rose, what's happened to you?" they asked her. "Please tell us." But she wouldn't say a word.

Every day was the same. They couldn't understand her silence. Their only consolation was that she seemed to be quite happy in her task of gathering nettles and weaving the flax she made from them, and when she finished her first coat of mail her eyes shone with joy.

One morning some hunters were riding by.

They saw the beautiful girl alone and busy at her task, and called their prince over to see her. He fell in love with her, and came every day to see her, just sitting by to watch her sewing.

"Come with me to the castle," he asked her. "Will you marry me?"

She said nothing at all to him, and he took her silence for consent and lifted her up on his horse. She could say nothing, only gaze up at the sky and hope that her brothers would see where she was going and come to find her there.

When they arrived at the castle the prince showed her to her room, and Snow-rose was overjoyed to see that her nettles and her weaving had been brought for her by one of the huntsmen. "This is to remind you of the kind of life you used to lead," the prince told her, and

was amused to see her sitting down straight to her task, as if nothing else mattered to her.

Everybody who saw Snow-rose loved her because of her beauty. Everyone, that is, except for the prince's mother. She was sure that the girl was a woodman's daughter, and she was furious that her son had brought a common speechless girl into her castle. "You're not good enough for him!" she hissed. "I'll show him how worthless you are!"

So when Snow-rose was bathing in the stream, the queen took three toads and told them to sit on the girl's head and neck and shoulders.

"Make her as ugly as you are!" she said to one, and to another, "Make her as sluggish as you are!" and to the third, "Make her as bad-tempered as you are and then the prince will hate her!" But the girl was too good and innocent for the magic spell to work on her, and as soon as the toads touched her they turned into red flowers and floated away.

And still Snow-rose wove her coats of mail, all day and all night, by moonlight and candlelight. Nothing would keep her from her task. Soon she had run out of nettles, and she took to leaving the castle at night in search of more. The very best nettles were in the graveyard. She knew that was where the witches liked to meet, around the newly dug graves, where it was said they would eat anyone, alive or dead.

Snow-rose was very frightened, yet she desperately needed the nettles, so she crept out there in the still of the night. But the queen saw the light of her candle through the window one night and decided to follow her, and when she saw her kneeling down in the graveyard surrounded by cackling witches she ran to the prince and woke him up.

"That girl you have brought home is a witch!" she said in triumph. "Come and see!" And the prince came and saw for himself the newly turned earth, and the ring of witches, and Snow-rose kneeling among them, and he had to believe what he saw. "If you are innocent, say so!" he begged her. Snow-rose said nothing.

"Then she must be guilty," the prince said, with sorrow in his heart.

"Throw her in jail!" the queen ordered.

Now in that country witches, if they were caught, were burnt to death, and that was the punishment that the wicked queen demanded for the girl. Snow-rose sat in her cell as silent as ever on her last night on this earth, and her nettles and weaving were flung in for her to sleep on. Nothing could have pleased her more. She had almost completed her task now. There was only one coat of mail to be sewn.

Just before dark she heard a flapping of wings outside the grating of her prison. She ran to the bars and saw her youngest brother there. She wanted to cry out to him for help, but she said nothing. He lifted his wings and flew away again.

Next morning a great fire had been prepared and she was led out to it on a cart. She had her coats of mail over her arm, and as the cart was being pulled along, she sewed. Right up to the time that she was drawn to the fire, she sewed as if nothing else mattered. Only one sleeve remained.

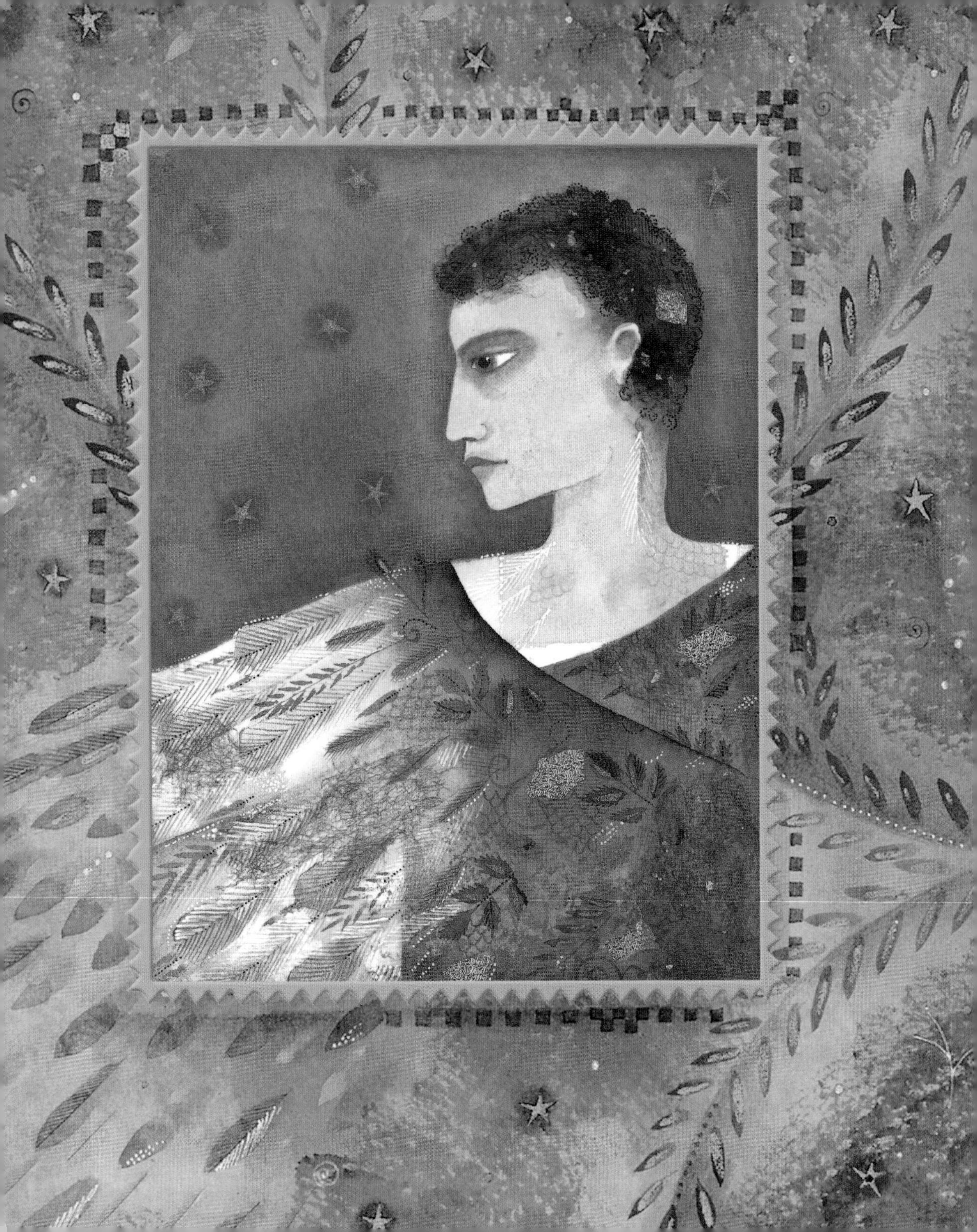

The crowd jeered. "Take her evil magic away from her!" they shouted.

But as they ran forward to seize the coats of mail there came a wild beating of wings around their heads, making the air turn cold as snow. The eleven swans circled round and the townspeople ducked and cowered and ran for shelter. Quickly Snow-rose threw the coats of mail over her brothers.

The spell was broken. Eleven young men stood beside her, and the youngest had a swan's wing instead of an arm.

Snow-rose stood up and faced her prince. "I am innocent," she said.

The bells of the town rang for seven days. The eleven brothers danced at the wedding of the prince and his bride, but the wicked queen wasn't there. Oh no. She had been thrown on the fire.

# About ✦ the ✦ Tales

I had a wonderful time choosing which stories to tell from among the hundreds that I read. Even the most familiar stories have echoes in many different cultures around the world, and the problem sometimes was to decide which version to model my story on. I tried to find the earliest written sources available, and from those, the ones with the most perfect shape. Among the tellers, writers and translators I worked from were the Brothers Grimm, Hans Christian Andersen, W. B. Yeats, A. N. Afanasiev, Charles Perrault and N. J. Dawood. I would also like to thank the children who listened with such encouragement and enthusiasm to my particular way of telling the tales: Lee, Liam, Tom, Matthew, Richard, Francis, Rosie, Katie, Amy, Alice, George and Alex of Edale Primary School.

## Tales first recorded by:

ALEXANDER N. AFANASIEV (1826–71)
*The Fire-Bird*

HANS CHRISTIAN ANDERSEN (1805–75)
*The Wild Swans*

ANTOINE GALLAND (1646–1715)
*Aladdin and the Enchanted Lamp*

JACOB GRIMM (1785–1863) AND WILHELM GRIMM (1786–1859)
*Cinderella (Ashputtel), The Frog Prince, Hansel and Gretel,
Little Red Riding Hood, Rapunzel, Rumpelstiltskin,
The Sleeping Beauty in the Forest, Snow White (Snowdrop)*

MADAME LE PRINCE DE BEAUMONT (1711–80)
*Beauty and the Beast*